FREDDY

and the

BASEBALL TEAM

from

MARS

FREDDY *and the*

BASEBALL
TEAM
from MARS

Walter R. Brooks

Illustrated by Kurt Wiese

A YEARLING BOOK

Published by
Dell Publishing Co., Inc.
1 Dag Hammarskjold Plaza
New York, New York 10017

Yearling ® TM 913705, Dell Publishing Co., Inc.

ISBN: 0-440-42724-X

Reprinted by arrangement with Alfred A. Knopf, Inc.
Printed in the United States of America

February 1984

10 9 8 7 6 5 4 3 2

CW

FREDDY

and the

BASEBALL TEAM

from

MARS

CHAPTER

1

It had been a hard winter and a late one. In early March the duck pond on the Bean farm had been frozen solid for six weeks. Nearly every afternoon Mr. Bean, an accomplished skater, had spent an hour or two on the ice, swooping about in loops and figure eights, with the ends of his muffler flying in the air behind him. Some of the farm animals sat in the snow on the bank and watched, applauding the more difficult and graceful figures; others, who had skates of their own, attempted to match Mr. Bean's feats—sometimes with pretty funny results.

Most of the larger animals skated on all fours, with a pair of skates on their forefeet and another pair on their hind feet. They couldn't do any figure skating, of course, but they could whiz round and round the pond at high speed. There wasn't room for many of them at a time; and when Hank, the old white horse, started off, the smaller animals scrambled for safety. Luckily for them, Hank never stayed out very long, and of the three cows, only Mrs. Wiggins liked skating, so there was generally room for everybody.

Except, of course, when some of the circus animals came up from Centerboro. Mr. Boomschmidt's circus was wintering in Centerboro this year—the first year they had stayed in the North—and every day or so a few of them would be up with their skates. Most of them weren't very good, though, and Hannibal, the elephant, although he had skates with double runners because his ankles were weak, finally had to be asked not to go on the pond when

there were others there, for if he fell, and a
duck or a rabbit was under him, the results
were quite serious.

One clear cold afternoon Freddy, the pig,
started up to the duck pond, carrying his skates.
The snow sparkled in the bright sun like mil-
lions of diamonds, and the ring of skates on ice
and the shouts of the skaters came down pleas-
antly to him. When he reached the pond, he
found nearly all the animals there. The ice was
crowded, and the bank was lined with spectators. Freddy sat down between Henrietta, the
hen, and her husband, Charles, the rooster, and
started to put on his skates.

"What are you two doing up here?" he
asked. "I thought you didn't like skating."

"We don't," Charles said. "But we have a
date to go tobogganing with Mac, and we like
to watch Mr. Bean, so we said for him to pick
us up here."

Mac was a wildcat who lived up in the Big
Woods. Many people would think it decidedly
foolhardy for two chickens to make a date with
a wildcat. But although the animals had at first
been suspicious of Mac, they had come finally to
trust in his good intentions. They could even
joke about their former fears. And when
Freddy said: "Well, it's nice to have known
you, Charles," the rooster said with a grin:

"Mac doesn't like chicken. I understand pork-and-beans is his dish."

Mr. Bean drifted by, skating backward. He took his pipe from his mouth and waved it at Freddy. "Want to waltz?" he called.

"Soon as I get my skates on," Freddy replied.

"He skates backward a lot," said Henrietta.

"He says he can manage his pipe better that way," Freddy explained. "Smoke doesn't get in his eyes."

"Can't see why he's never set those whiskers afire," Charles said. "All the years I've known him I've never seen him without that pipe, and my goodness, it's so short and his whiskers are so bushy sometimes you can't see the pipe at all; it looks like a brush fire."

"Maybe he's had 'em fireproofed or something," Freddy said. He got up and glided out onto the ice. He had on a red knitted cap with a tassel and an old sports coat of Mr. Bean's. This of course roused no comment, for it was his usual skating costume. The coat was not long enough to cover his tail, which curled out from under it. But today that tail was not, as usual, faintly pink with the cold. It had a little knitted sweater on, and the sweater was red, to match his cap.

A shout of laughter went up from the bank he had just left, and as he started to circle the

"What's the matter with your tail?"

pond, Jinx, the black cat, swung up beside him. Jinx, having a warm coat of his own fur, didn't need a skating costume, but he wore a red beret, for style. Like Freddy, he was a good skater and skated upright on his hind legs.

"Hi, pig," he said. "What's the matter with your tail—you sprain it?"

Freddy said: "My tail hasn't got fur on it, like yours. It gets cold. I knitted that tail-muff myself—Mrs. Bean showed me how. It makes a lot of difference, let me tell you."

"I should think you'd just let it freeze, and then break it off. You wouldn't have to bother trying to keep it warm . . . hey, look out!" and he swung Freddy to one side as Mrs. Wiggins, with all four skates in the air, came slithering across the ice, upsetting several rabbits who weren't quick enough in getting out of the way.

Freddy and Mr. Bean helped the cow up, but she was laughing so hard that she fell right down again. "Thanks," she said, "but you better just leave me here until I get my legs sorted out. My sakes, I was trying to cut a figure eight, but my front legs started on one loop and my hind legs started on the other, and I guess it's a mercy I fell down. If I'd kept on you'd never have got me untangled."

So they left her, and Freddy and Mr. Bean waltzed. To keep time, Mr. Bean sang what he said was the *Blue Danube* waltz. It wasn't a very pretty tune, for it went all on one note: "*Tum*, tum, tum, *Tum*, tum, tum,"—Mr. Bean wasn't a very good singer. And every time he said "*Tum*," a puff of smoke came out of the whiskers and swirled up Freddy's nose. He was too polite to say anything about it, but pretty soon he began to feel queer. "Guess I'll have to sit down," he said. "Getting dizzy."

He went over and collapsed on the bank, and Mr. Bean went out to the middle of the pond and began writing his name on the ice. Gradually all the animals stopped skating to watch. He made the final n, then said: "Now I'll make the period." And he swung his arms out wide and began spinning. He spun so fast that he was just a blur, and the sparks flew from his pipe and made a circle of fire around his head.

"Gosh, Freddy," Jinx said, "get a load of the human pinwheel!"

Freddy had been sitting with his eyes shut. He lifted his head and opened one eye, then shut it quickly and groaned. "Oh dear, does he have to do that?"

"Hey!" Jinx exclaimed. "I bet his whiskers are burning! Look, Freddy, they're . . . oh no, they're all right. Golly, they must be made of asbestos!"

Freddy opened a cautious eye again. But Mr. Bean had stopped whirling. He was kneeling on one knee with both arms outspread, as the animals cheered his performance. Then slowly he took the pipe out of his mouth and tapped it on the ice. It was empty. The wind of his whirling had sucked every shred of burning tobacco out of the bowl.

Freddy now joined in the applause. He didn't feel so sick and dizzy now that Mr. Bean was standing still, but it still made him a little giddy to watch the others circling the pond. Most of them glided slowly along, but John, the fox, and Georgie, the little brown dog, were racing. They zipped in and out, bending low with their forepaws clasped behind them. Mr. Bean was now sitting on the bank. He was watching them, frowning a little.

"They hadn't ought to race when the pond's so crowded," said Henrietta. "I'd like to give that John a piece of my mind."

"Don't bankrupt yourself," said Jinx with a grin, and skated off before she could fly at him.

"Fresh cat!" said the hen indignantly. "Oh, look, Freddy! Now they've done it!"

Alice and Emma, the two ducks, had been

skating sedately together at the end of the pond. They wore little roller skates which Mr. Bean's Uncle Ben had made for them. For their Uncle Wesley, who lived with them, felt that rollers were more ladylike. "And there *is* something masculine about regular ice skates, isn't there?" said Alice. "Uncle Wesley is so sensitive to these things!"

"Dear Uncle Wesley!" said Emma.

So they were skating along, wing and wing, and watching half a dozen rabbits who were playing snap-the-whip. The whip snapped just as the two racers came scooting around the end of the pond. Two rabbits were snapped off; one slid straight into John, who crashed over him; Georgie dodged the other and ran smack into the two ducks, upsetting them and sending them slithering across the ice, quacking indignantly, roller skates in the air.

"Georgie!" Mr. Bean got up. "Get off the ice!" He jerked a thumb down toward the farmhouse. "You too, fox." He spoke quietly, but the two went over to the bank, took off their skates, and trotted off. "Can't have that sort of thing," Mr. Bean said. He looked down at Freddy. "Care to waltz?" he asked, as he took out his tobacco pouch and started to refill his pipe.

"Oh," said Freddy weakly, "yes, I—I guess so."

Fortunately for him, a sudden burst of laughter from the other side of the pond drew Mr. Bean's attention. He skated over to where a crowd of animals was gathering around a strange little black creature about two feet high, who seemed to be showing them a white envelope. The creature had a round body and a pear-shaped head with long feelers on it. He had two spindly legs and four spindly arms and looked rather like a spider, except that he had three eyes, the middle one set between and above the other two.

"Why, it's old Two-clicks!" Freddy exclaimed, and skated quickly across toward him. For Two-clicks (that was what his name sounded like in his own language) was the leader of the five Martians who had come spinning down in their flying saucer last summer and landed in the Centerboro fairgrounds not far from the Bean farm. Mr. Boomschmidt's Stupendous and Unexcelled Circus was giving shows at the fairgrounds, and the Martians, after adventures which have been related elsewhere, had decided to stay on earth and join the circus.*

---

* FREDDY AND THE MEN FROM MARS

"He's got a letter from Mr. Boom," Hank said as Freddy came up. "But it hasn't got a regular address on it; it just says 'Freddy is queer.' " He laughed, and all the others joined him. " 'Freddy is queer,' hey?" they said. "Ain't it the truth! Freddy, old Boom's onto you at last."

"What are you talking about?" said the pig. "Hello, Two-clicks. What's all this about?" And then he repeated his greeting in Martian, for these strangers from another world had spent a lot of time on the farm, and he had learned to talk a little with them in their own language, a queer combination of chirps and clicks and squeaks.

Two-clicks held out the envelope. "That doesn't say 'Freddy is queer,' you dopes," the pig said. "It's addressed to 'Freddy, *Esquire*.' 'Esquire' is just a fancy way of saying 'Mister.' "

"Fancy nothing!" said Jinx. "It's a good plain way of saying what Mr. Boom thinks about you."

"Yeah, they're wise to you at last, pig," said Hank.

Freddy didn't answer. He was reading the letter. "Hey," he said, "listen to this! We've got to do something about this." And he read:

Centerboro
Tuesday

DEAR FRIEND FREDDY:

I hope this finds you as it leaves me, in good health and spirits. Although my goodness, my spirits aren't so good either. Because we are in trouble. Squeak-squeak, one of our Martians, has been kidnapped. At least he's disappeared, and his brothers —if they are his brothers—are awful upset about it. We called the police in, but of course the cops can't speak Martian, and so the other Martians couldn't tell them much. And anyway, the police chief says they're nothing but bugs, and he's got something better to do than hunt for a missing bug. So I got Two-clicks to take this note up to you in his flying saucer, and if you are not too busy would you please come down to town with him and help us find Squeak-squeak?

Your friend,

ORESTES P. BOOMSCHMIDT

"Well, I guess I'd better go," said Freddy. "How'd you get here, Two-clicks?" And he repeated the question in Martian. It sounded like this: "Clickety-squeak chirp, chirp-chirp chickle, chickle click squeakity-click."

Two-click's answer sounded like somebody using a very old typewriter which badly needed oiling.

"H'm," said Freddy. "If I understand him, he came up in the flying saucer. Left it in the Big Woods. I wish you spoke more English, Two-clicks."

Two-clicks said: "Me . . . speak . . . English." He pointed to the pig. "Freddick, Detectick. Quick-quick."

"Sure, you speak it fine," said Mr. Bean. "Like a native." He made the fizzing sound that meant that he was laughing behind his whiskers. "Native of Bongo-Bongo, I guess." Then he turned to Freddy. "Well, you're the detective; go ahead and detect. Go pack your suitcase."

CHAPTER

2

The winter headquarters of Boomschmidt's Stupendous & Unexcelled Circus was usually in Virginia, but this year, partly because the animals had so many friends in Centerboro, and partly because they had never had a chance to try any winter sports, they had voted to spend the winter in the North. Centerboro was of course only a few miles from the Bean farm, and the circus was encamped in the baseball park just outside the town. Mr. Boomschmidt and his wife, who was Mademoiselle Rose, the bareback rider, and his mother, who spent all her time knitting him fancy waistcoats that didn't fit, lived in a little house with a big picture window at the edge of the ball park. Here they could sit and look out through the window at the wagons where the animals lived, all drawn up in a circle; and they could watch the various performers practicing their acts, in preparation for the coming season.

All the performers in the big tent were animals except Mlle Rose and Mr. Hercules, Mr. Boomschmidt's brother, a huge man who looked just like Mr. Boomschmidt blown up to three times life size. Mr. Hercules did weight lifting and some juggling. He wasn't very bright. Old Mrs. Boomschmidt said she guessed all his brains had gone to muscles. "Takes after his father," she said. "He could lift a five-hundred-pound sack of gold coins with one hand, but he wouldn't have known what to do with it if he had."

It took the flying saucer only a few seconds to cover the four or five miles between the farm and Centerboro. Freddy had Two-clicks bring it around up to the back door, where it hovered for a minute so that he could step from it right into the house, without having anybody but the Boomschmidts know that he'd come. Mr. Boomschmidt was delighted to see him, and kept patting him on the back and saying: "My goodness, it's good to see you, Freddy! My goodness gracious me, now we'll have Squeak-squeak back home in two shakes!" And Mlle Rose and old Mrs. Boomschmidt rushed out into the kitchen, from which came a rattle of crockery and a crashing of pots and pans, and pretty soon they came back with an enormous chocolate cake smothered in whipped cream, and a big pot of cocoa.

Mrs. Boomschmidt helped Freddy to cake. "We're very happy to have you here, Freddy," she said. "Very happy." And Freddy noticed that tears were running down her cheeks as she smiled at him.

"Now, now, Mother!" said Mr. Boomschmidt, and to Freddy he said: "Mother always cries when she's happy."

"My goodness," said Freddy, "but that doesn't leave you anything to do when you're *un*happy, ma'am."

"Oh, I cry then, too," said Mrs. Boomschmidt, wiping her eyes.

Leo, the lion, and two elephants had even taken up golf.

Freddy shook his head. "But—but how does anybody know. . . ." he began.

"They don't," said Mr. Boomschmidt.

Freddy gave it up. "Well, I'm glad you're happy today anyway, ma'am. And now, how about Squeak-squeak?"

There wasn't much to tell. At first, to keep them from being mobbed whenever they appeared in public, the Martians hadn't been allowed to go into town by themselves. But after the people had got used to them, they were free, like all the circus animals, to go where they pleased. In Centerboro, as in other communities where they were well known, the animals entered into the town's social life. They were invited everywhere; several of them had joined the Centerboro Country Club; Andrew, the hippopotamus, was a member of Rotary; and Leo, the lion, and two of the elephants had even taken up golf. It was not at all unusual to glance in a lighted window in the evening and see a tiger dining with the family, or Willy, the boa constrictor, taking a hand at the bridge table. And so the Martians, since they had nice manners, and in addition were curiosities from another planet, were made much of. Now that they could understand, and even speak a little English, they hardly dined at home one evening a week.

Three days ago Squeak-squeak had had dinner at the home of a Mr. Henry Avalanche. After a pleasant evening of tiddlywinks, the guest had started home. At nine thirty he had stopped at a store two blocks from the ball park and bought a bag of freshly roasted peanuts, of which all the Martians were very fond. But he had never reached home. Somewhere between the peanut store and the ball park he had disappeared.

"Was there no trail of peanut shells leading from the store in any direction?" Freddy asked.

"That's what we looked for," said Mr. Boomschmidt. "Because you can trail the Martians all over town that way. They're always eating peanuts and throwing the shucks away. There wasn't a trace."

"What makes you think he was kidnapped?" Freddy asked.

"My goodness, he wouldn't have left town without telling the other Martians. And if he'd had an accident, we'd have heard."

"What can you do, Freddy?" Mlle Rose asked eagerly.

"I'll have to think about it a little before I answer that question," Freddy said, putting on his Great Detective expression, which made him look almost cross-eyed with determination. Indeed he hadn't the faintest idea what to do. But that was almost always so at the beginning of a case. The great thing was not to let his client know how hopeless he felt. He knew that if his cases were finally solved, it was more by luck than by brilliance. But he'd always been lucky. He would stall along, and sooner or later would come the lucky break.

He sat eating his third piece of cake and looking out the window at the circus encampment. An elephant went by carrying a pail of water. He kicked up the snow with his big feet. "I bet that tail of his is cold," Freddy thought. "I bet he'd like a tail-muff like mine." Mr. Hercules came out of his trailer and began taking his afternoon exercise, juggling ten-pound cannonballs. Two alligators stopped to watch him, then one said something in the other's ear, and they both began to giggle and walked on. On the other side of the row of wagons four of the Martians were playing catch. They never seemed to mind the cold, and never wore gloves or overcoats. Leaning on the fence and watching them were a dozen or so boys and men. One of them, a tall, burly man with a red face, looked familiar to Freddy. He stared at him for a minute, but couldn't place him, and then Mr. Boomschmidt said:

"You know, when we get Squeak-squeak back, I'd like to find something for the Martians to do in the big tent. I don't think they're contented being just a side show and sitting around having people stare at them. They want to get into the act. Maybe you could think of something, Freddy."

One of the Martians had just reached up and caught a high fast ball. He caught it with three hands, but used only one to send it whizzing on to the player on his left.

"Looks like a regular baseball they're playing with," Freddy said. "Do they play like this often?"

"Herc got 'em interested in it," said Mr. Boomschmidt. "He used to play professional ball, you know. Pitched one season for Pittsburgh. But he was too strong. No catcher could hold his fast ball. And my gracious, when he hit one he knocked the cover right off. I guess he got kind of disgusted; he said it was a sissy game, and quit. He said if they'd play it with cannonballs and iron bats it might be worth playing."

Freddy had been watching the Martians. "You know," he said, "they're pretty good. They're fast, and they're accurate. Say, why couldn't you organize them into a baseball team? Get games with the local ball clubs in the towns where you give shows. Look—watch that one throw—I think it's Chirp-squeak. He threw with his upper left arm last time, now he's using his lower right one. Boy, what a pitcher you could make out of him! Yeah, and now he's using his lower left. Can you see how balled up a batter would get if he didn't know which of four arms a pitcher was going to use?"

"Golly!" said Mr. Boomschmidt. "I think you've got something, Freddy. Yes sir, I do! Only—hey! Wait a minute! How do we know they can hit?"

"I don't care whether they can or not," Freddy said.

"Well but, Freddy—we got to get hits to win games."

"We've got to get *runs,*" said the pig.

"Why, sure we have, but—"

"Look," said Freddy, "you help me to organize this team and I'll guarantee you the runs. Now we've got five Martians. Four if Squeak-squeak doesn't get back. Who else have you got to fill out your team?"

"Well," said Mr. Boomschmidt modestly, "of course there's me—"

Old Mrs. Boomschmidt said: "Orestes used to be a real good player. If there was a whole pane of glass in the neighborhood, even if it was two houses down and around the corner, he could put the ball right through the middle of it."

"Now, Mother," said Mr. Boomschmidt. "Let's let bygones be bygones, specially when they're thirty-year-old ones. Well, now, I think we can scrape up enough talent to fill out a team. There's me, and there's the ostrich, Oscar. Ever see him throw a stone? He throws underhand, like he was bowling—or maybe it's underfoot, because he throws with a claw. He can catch, too, though not the high ones. He'd be good at shortstop.

"Then there's Leo. He played softball one winter down in Florida. So did the two elephants. Old Hannibal, he never used a bat—used to swing at 'em with his trunk. He could throw with that trunk, too. Oh, my gracious, Freddy, I believe we could get up an Interplanetary League. Teams from Mars and Venus and Neptune and the rest of 'em—and earth of course—and—"

"Hey, wait a minute!" Freddy interrupted. "You're so far ahead of me you're out of sight. Let's just stick to Mars vs. Centerboro, and Mars vs. Tushville, and so on—"

"And Squeak-squeak," said Mlle Rose.

"I hadn't forgotten Squeak-squeak," Freddy said. "I think the first thing—"

Mr. Boomschmidt interrupted him. "Excuse me, Freddy," he said, jumping up, "I think I'll have a talk right now with Leo and Herc—see if we can't organize a team."

"But look, Mr. Boom," Freddy said, and then stopped, for Mr. Boomschmidt had bounced right out of the room.

"He's always like that when he gets a new idea," said Mlle Rose.

"I know," Freddy said. "No use trying to talk to him about Squeak-squeak now. Well, I guess—" He stopped suddenly. The tall, red-faced man who had been watching the Martians had turned and looked toward the house, and Freddy recognized him. "That man!" he exclaimed, drawing back from the window. "Now, why's he up here? He's a real estate man, E. H. Anderson—Mr. Eha, we used to call him. And I never knew him to be interested in anything he couldn't make money out of."

"You know him?" Mlle Rose asked.

"Good heavens, I should say I did! He haunted houses."

The two women laughed, and Mrs. Boomschmidt said: "He's a pretty robust ghost. If he tries to seep through a keyhole or under a door he's going to need a lot of help."

"Just the same, he was pretty good at it. He

had a lot of masks and luminous paint and stuff, and then he had a gang of rats to help him: Simon's gang. I guess you've heard of them.

"It was a racket with Mr. Eha. He'd give out that a house was haunted, and then he'd make it so unpleasant for the folks that lived there that they'd leave. When they tried to sell the house, he'd scare away everybody that came to look at it. Then he'd offer them about a quarter of what it was worth, and by that time they'd be glad to take whatever they could, and they'd sell. He tried that on a hotel up on Otesaraga Lake, and he was going to work it on Mr. Bean's house. But we broke up his gang."

"Well, do you think he could have had anything to do with kidnapping Squeak-squeak?" Mlle Rose asked.

"I wouldn't think so," said Freddy. "He's not a kidnapper. But it's funny, just the same. I'd better find out what he's up to. I don't want anybody to know I'm here. I'll get into a disguise and follow him."

CHAPTER

3

Freddy had more than twenty disguises that he used in his detective work. The trouble with most of them was that they didn't disguise him much. When he got them on he wasn't Dr. Hopper, or old Mrs. O'Brien; he was just a pig in a derby hat and a false mustache, or a pig in a bonnet and shawl. They were really more bother than they were worth.

However, a really good disguise is a great help in detective work, and he had at last got together an outfit that he thought a pig could wear successfully. There was a long, black old-fashioned coat of the kind known as a Prince Albert. It was the one Mr. Bean had been married in, but the moths had got into it and Mrs. Bean had thrown it out. She said she couldn't feel sentimental about a lot of old moth holes.

The black trousers were too long, but they fell in wrinkles at the bottom and helped to hide his trotters. He had an old shapeless felt hat and a white wig and a long white beard, which made his nose look shorter, and he wore spectacles that had belonged to Mrs. Bean's father, who was very near-sighted. They really did disguise Freddy, because a pig's eyes are much smaller than a man's, and these glasses had very thick lenses, and magnified his eyes so they looked twice as big.

But one thing Freddy had forgotten. It hadn't occurred to him that while the thick lenses made his eyes look different to other people, they also made everything look different to him. The ground seemed to be right up under his nose, and everything more than a few feet off was so blurred and distorted that he couldn't tell what it was. So when, with a corncob pipe in his mouth and a cane in his hand, he started over to join the group of people watching the Martians, he tripped and stumbled at every other step, and he had to lift the glasses up, finally, to see where he was going.

But when he had worked his way through the little crowd until he was close to Mr. Anderson, he had to leave the spectacles in place. "Golly," he said to himself, "I'm glad I've got this cane. I'd have fallen on my face and busted the darn glasses by this time if I hadn't. I bet I look a hundred years old, tottering along. But that's how I want to look." Something loomed up ahead of him. "Wonder if that's Anderson. It's the right color, but it looks more like a kangaroo. Oops!" he said out loud. "Excuse me, mister." For he had misjudged the distance and walked right into the man.

"Hey, look where you're going, Grampa," said Mr. Anderson irritably.

Freddy had decided to be sort of a bad-tempered old man. So now he said in a high, piping, irritable voice that he thought would go well with his get-up: "Well, I said excuse me, didn't I? What ye want me to do, sonny— write ye out an apology?"

Anderson gave a laugh which was good-humored in a bullying sort of way. "Well, to begin with," he said, "you might get off my foot."

Freddy stepped back hastily. "Consarn ye," he snapped. "D'ye have to spread your great feet all over the landscape?"

Anderson laughed again. "Now, now," he said. "It was me that got stepped on, after all."

Freddy thought they'd better get off the subject of feet. He didn't want to call attention to the fact that his were trotters. He flourished his stick out toward the ball-playing Martians, knocking off the cap of a boy standing beside him. "What are all them little critters?" he asked, though all he could see of the Martians was a lot of little black specks floating around in the distance. They looked like tadpoles swimming to and fro in his glasses.

"Take it easy with that stick," Anderson said, "before you put someone's eye out." Then he said: "You a stranger here? Haven't you heard about the people from Mars that landed here in a flying saucer and joined Boom-schmidt's circus?"

"Heard some folderol about 'em," said Freddy. "Fakes, ain't they?"

Mr. Anderson said on the contrary, they were the real thing. And he told Freddy about them.

"Tcha!" said Freddy. "Don't believe a word of it!"

Mr. Anderson didn't say anything. Freddy leaned with both fore-trotters on the handle of his stick and looked out at the blurred landscape. Then he said: "You acquainted around here?"

"More or less," said the other. "What do you want to know?"

"Well, I'll tell you." Freddy peered up at the red face. "They got a good bank in this town?"

"Sure, they got a fine bank. Why? You want to stick it up?"

"I ain't sayin' I wouldn't like to if I was forty years younger," Freddy said with a wheezy cackle that he thought went well with his white whiskers. "No, sir, I ain't ambitious. All I want is a safe place to keep my savings. Like to lost 'em a week ago. House burned down. But I saved the money." He tapped his breast pocket significantly. "Now I got to have a place to put it till I get me another place to live."

Mr. Anderson moved a little closer and Freddy could feel his suddenly aroused interest. "Now I've hooked him," he thought. "But what'll I do with him? He isn't likely to have anything more to do with Squeak-squeak's disappearance than any of the other people out here watching the Martians." Then he thought: "Oh well, I might as well have a little fun."

"Don't like carryin' all my cash around in my pocket," he said.

"I should think not!" said Anderson. "Want me to walk down to the bank with you? Only —well, why not invest your money instead of letting it lie idle in a bank? Of course, if it's only a few hundred—" He paused, but Freddy didn't say anything. "why then," he went on, "the bank's all right. But if you've got enough to buy, say, a house. . . . Well," he said with a laugh, "I'm a real estate man, and naturally I'd boost real estate as an investment. I know houses you can buy with as little as a thousand down, and then you can rent 'em and make good money. How much did you say you had, Mr. Ah—"

"Arquebus is the name," said Freddy. "Henry Arquebus. And I didn't say."

"Quite right," Mr. Anderson agreed heartily. "Shouldn't have asked you. Only thing, I was thinking of a little piece of property I've got right now. Prettiest little house you ever saw. It cost this fellow eighteen thousand, and he'll sell for cash for— But forgive me, I get so enthusiastic about bargains like this. If I only had the money I'd buy it myself.

"However, you want to go to the bank. Come along and I'll show you."

So he accompanied Freddy down to the bank. Freddy stumbled a lot, and once he walked into a lamp post and tipped his hat and apologized to it. So Mr. Anderson took his arm. But Freddy shook the guiding hand off, for at the same time that it was steadying his uncertain feet, he could feel cautious fingers exploring to see if he had a well-stuffed wallet in his breast pocket. And of course the pocket was empty.

Although at the bank Anderson rather insisted on coming in, Freddy refused. "I don't need ye, mister," he said. "And folks that keep pokin' their noses into my business likely'll get 'em singed. Or chawed off." He cackled. "I ain't particular which."

"I can see you aren't," said Mr. Anderson good-naturedly. "Well, let me give you my card, and if you decide to put any of that money into real estate, just let me show you what I've got." He tucked the card into Freddy's right-hand pocket, and Freddy could feel that he was making sure that there wasn't a wallet in that pocket either. "Where are you staying in town?" he asked.

"No harm in telling you," Freddy said. "Got a room at Mis' Peppercorn's."

"Oh, yes, I know Mrs. Peppercorn," said Anderson. "You won't mind if I drop in one day when I'm passing by? Just for a little chat. Frankly, I like you, Mr. Arquebus."

"Well, some folks do," said Freddy, and went into the bank.

From the window he watched Mr. Anderson. The man stood around for a minute as if undecided, then seemed to come to a decision, and walked off hurriedly. As soon as he was out of sight, Freddy started back to the ball park.

On the way, he stopped in to see old Mrs. Peppercorn. He knew that she sometimes rented her spare room, and although at first he hadn't intended to really stay there, he decided that it might be a good idea. He could move around on his detective work more safely than if he stayed with the Boomschmidts, for he didn't want the circus animals or the Centerboro people to know that he was looking for Squeak-squeak. But Mrs. Peppercorn was an old and trusted friend.

She came to the door. At first Freddy had thought he'd pretend to be Mr. Arquebus, to find out if she could see through his disguise. But she had a fiery temper, and she didn't like to be fooled. She might laugh about it with him afterward, but at the time she was as likely

as not to chase him up the street with a broom.
So he just said: "Mrs. P., I'm Freddy. I'm
working on a case. Can I come in?"

Well, she stared at him a full minute, and
then she started to laugh. She laughed so loud
and so long that Freddy saw a lace curtain
tremble in Mrs. Lafayette Bingle's front window across the street, and he knew Mrs. Bingle
had heard and was peeking out. So he took Mrs.
Peppercorn by the arm and pulled her inside
and shut the door.

Mrs. Peppercorn screeched a good deal when
she laughed. It wasn't a pretty laugh, but it was
infectious—which means that when you heard
it you began laughing yourself, even if you
didn't know what she was laughing about.
Freddy's laugh was infectious too, so the harder
one laughed the harder the other one did, and
pretty soon they were both yelling until the
windows shook, and I don't know what would
have happened if Freddy, in trying to get his
breath, hadn't given a sort of gasp and drawn a
lot of the white whiskers into his mouth and
halfway down his throat. Of course he choked,
and Mrs. Peppercorn had to help him and
pound him on the back, and by the time he got
his breath back they had got over laughing.

"Good land, Freddy," Mrs. Peppercorn said,
"you know when I opened that door—well,

Mrs. Peppercorn had to pound him on the back.

you're the livin' image of Great-uncle Ezra Pocus, who's been dead and gone forty years."

"I should think you'd have been scared, instead of laughing," Freddy said.

"Why, you would, wouldn't you?" said Mrs. Peppercorn, looking surprised. "I guess it's those whiskers. I— Oh, don't get me started again. Who are you detecting, Freddy?"

So Freddy explained about the disappearance of Squeak-squeak. "But I sort of got off the track fooling around with Mr. Anderson," he said. "Though I'm just curious to know what kind of a crooked deal he's stewing up for poor Mr. Henry Arquebus."

"You'd better forget it," she said. "Ed Anderson is bad medicine." A look of pleased surprise came across her face. "Bless me, that's almost a rhyme!"

"It is—one of *your* rhymes," said Freddy sourly. As a poet himself, he highly disapproved of Mrs. Peppercorn's efforts in that line. For to make one word rhyme with another, she would twist it all out of shape. Freddy had sent her a valentine once which used all of her kind of rhymes. It began:

> *Mrs. Peppercorn's a votary*
> *Of the muse. That is: a poet.*

She's written the finest potary
That anyone ever wro-et.

But Mrs. Peppercorn thought this a very good verse, and congratulated Freddy heartily on having changed over to her style of writing.

Right now Freddy didn't want to get into an argument about poetry. So he said: "I expect you're right about Anderson. And if he's up to anything, it'll be haunting houses, not kidnapping Martians. But how about renting me that front room of yours for a few days? It'll be better making my headquarters here instead of at the circus."

So Mrs. Peppercorn said she'd be glad to have him, and Freddy went back to the ball park to get his bag.

CHAPTER

4

The Boomschmidts said they were sorry Freddy wasn't going to stay with them, but they agreed that if he did, they couldn't possibly keep his presence a secret. So he said he'd keep them posted on whatever he detected, and picked up his bag and stumbled out.

The space encircled by the circus wagons was empty now, a white snowy expanse, crisscrossed by the tracks of a dozen different animals. "Golly, I'd forgotten about tracks!" Freddy thought, and he went across to where he had stood beside Mr. Anderson. There were Anderson's prints, the soles with a sort of herringbone pattern, and the heels with a triangle in the middle. And next to them were the unmistakable prints of a pig's trotters.

"I wonder if he noticed," Freddy thought. "No, I'm sure he didn't. If he'd known Mr. Arquebus was a pig, he'd have known the pig was me, and boy, he'd have chased me from here all the way back to the farm. But I'll have to be careful, with this snow on the ground."

He started on toward the wagon where the Martians lived, when a ferocious roar behind him stopped him in his tracks. "Hey, you!" He turned and peered over his spectacles to see a large lion with a very curly mane trotting toward him across the snow.

It was Leo, one of Freddy's oldest and most trusted friends, and Freddy grinned behind his whiskers. Here was someone to try out his disguise on, but good!

"Where you going with that suitcase?" the lion demanded.

"I'm goin' about my business," Freddy

snapped, "and suppose you go on about yours."

"I am, mister," said the lion. "My business is with that suitcase, which has the initials F.B. on it, and which I recognize as belonging to my friend Freddy. Frederick Bean."

"That's what *you* say," Freddy replied. "Look, my frowzy-headed friend, why don't you run along home and catch mice?" And he started on.

But with a bound Leo was in front of him. Freddy was sorry that he couldn't see the lion's expression through his glasses. Leo spent a large part of his salary on his mane, and it was plain that he had recently had a permanent, so that to call him frowzy-headed was to hit him where it hurt most. And on top of that, to suggest to the king of beasts that he go home and catch mice! This time he let out a roar that brought a dozen animals tumbling out of their houses. "Well, dye my hair! You know who you're talking to, you bug-eyed old thief? Now put down that suitcase, or I'll comb those white whiskers for you with this." And he held up one enormous paw, with the three-inch claws extended, close under Freddy's nose.

Freddy knew that no matter how mad Leo was he would never hurt an old man, and he was trying to think up another good insult, when Mr. Boomschmidt came hurrying out.

"My goodness gracious, what's all this shouting? Do please lower your voice, Leo. Now, now; put those claws back, too. But what's this?" He took hold of the big paw. "You've been to that beauty shop again and had your claws painted. What's the color this time?"

Leo looked embarrassed. He turned his head aside. "Shell pink," he muttered.

"Really?" Mr. Boomschmidt was pleased. "How nice. What a pretty name. And a very pretty color, too. Don't you think so, Mr.—ah, Arquebus?"

Freddy grinned. When two of his animals got into an argument Mr. Boomschmidt always managed to lead the discussion off around a corner somewhere so that pretty soon the arguers were talking about something entirely different. Then he'd get them to agree about the new subject, and before long they would forget what they had disagreed about. He had a lot of tricks like that. And it tickled Freddy to see him working one on Leo, who knew him so well.

"Paint 'em baby blue for all of me," Freddy grated. "And wear rosebuds in his mane. Just so he minds his own business, no matter how silly."

Quite a crowd of animals had gathered, and one of the alligators giggled. Leo growled angrily and started to say something, but Mr.

Boomschmidt said: "Now, now, Leo; Mr. Arquebus is only trying to be helpful. Not that I think rosebuds would be entirely suitable—"

"You mean, you know this guy, chief?" Leo asked.

"Good grief, I should say so! Known him for years."

"Well, why couldn't you have said so?" Leo demanded. "I saw he had Freddy's suitcase and I thought he'd swiped it somewhere."

"Now be reasonable, Leo," said Mr. Boomschmidt. "How could I tell you everybody I've known for years? Well, good gracious, I suppose I could. But it will take some time. Suppose we begin with the— No, let's begin with the B's, since my name is Boomschmidt, and I've known myself for years. Well, there's Mr. Boomschmidt, here, and there's William F. Bean, and there's Bannister, Mr. Camphor's butler, and there's Walter R. Brooks who I'm told is writing another volume of his monumental work on the history of the Bean farm. And there's an old school friend, Mr. Arthur Bandersnatch. And there's Mr. Beller, in Beller & Rohr's music store. And there's George Birdseed, though maybe I ought not to count him, because he owes me two dollars. And there's—"

"All right, chief; all *right!*" said Leo. "I can take a hint without having the whole tele-

"Good grief—known him for years."

phone book thrown at me. I just hope Freddy knows that this old buzzard is walking around with his good suitcase, that's all! Buzzard. That begins with B, too, please note," he added. Then he stalked off.

"Break it up, animals," said Mr. Boomschmidt, and the listeners wandered away, looking back curiously over their shoulders at Freddy. "You hadn't ought to play tricks on Leo," Mr. Boomschmidt said. "Not when you don't want anybody to know you're here. Leo's smart; I bet he recognized you."

"I don't think so. If he had, he couldn't have resisted taking a really personal crack at me— I mean, something about pigs, or detectives, or poets. But anyway, I can trust him, and I want to have a talk with him later. I want to see the Martians first, though—see what they can tell me about Squeak-squeak."

"I came out to tell you, Freddy," Mr. Boomschmidt said. "They—they don't want to see you. I mean, just a few minutes ago Two-clicks came in and said never mind about Squeaksqueak; they knew where he was, and it was all right. No cause to worry."

Freddy frowned. "Did they tell you where he was?"

Mr. Boomschmidt said no, they wouldn't tell him anything.

Freddy stared at him. "I don't get it," he said. "They want me to come; they even get you to write a letter so as to be sure I'll come. Two-clicks was awful worried—I could tell. Now Squeak-squeak isn't back, but they aren't worried any more, and they want me to go home. What happened to change them?"

Mr. Boomschmidt said: "I don't know. You know, I went to talk to them about this base-ball business. They wouldn't talk about that; they wanted to know what you were doing about Squeak-squeak. But my goodness, half an hour later, after I'd talked to Herc and Leo, I went out to speak to them about it again. They were all looking at a big sheet of paper covered with those Martian duck tracks. They kind of pushed it one side and it was then they told me Squeak-squeak was all right. I bet if you could get a look at that paper—"

"You think it was a letter from Squeak-squeak?" Freddy asked. "But I can't read Martian anyway."

"I don't know what it was," said Mr. Boom-schmidt. "But I know that they *were* worried, more than ever, even though they said they weren't. They were worried because they were afraid you'd keep on trying to find Squeak-squeak, and they were worried about something else. Don't ask *me* what it is! That's your job."

"But if they want me to leave—"

"Look, Freddy," said Mr. Boomschmidt, "they're in pretty serious trouble, I'm sure. So even if they say they don't want you to, I think you ought to stay and get to the bottom of it. Now, suppose I tell them you've gone. Then I won't say any more about Squeak-squeak, but I'll get 'em interested in this baseball team. They're interested already, even though they're so worried. And I'll tell 'em that I've engaged a coach to get the team going. And you'll stay on as Mr. Arquebus and be the coach."

"Heck, Mr. Boom," Freddy said, "do I look like a coach in this rig?"

"You don't look like anything I ever saw before, and that's a fact," said Mr. Boomschmidt. "But what do Martians know about coaches? If I tell 'em you're a coach, then you're a coach. Come on, I'll go introduce you to 'em now."

The Martians were pleased to meet Mr. Arquebus, and seemed interested in learning to play baseball. Click Two-squeaks spoke for them. He spoke fairly good English, although of course with a strong Martian accent. This is impossible to reproduce on paper, and we will not try. And indeed he only said that they thought baseball would be fun, and that they would be ready to go out for practice whenever Mr. Arquebus sent for them.

"I thought there was one more of you," Freddy said.

Click Two-squeaks said there was, but he was away.

"We'll need him," said Freddy. "We've got to have at least nine, and with Mr. Boom and Mr. Hercules and Leo and Oscar and Hannibal, that's still only a bare team. You expect him back soon?"

The Martians rolled their three eyes at one another and Click Two-squeaks said uncertainly that they hoped so.

As they left the wagon where the Martians lived, Freddy stopped suddenly. "Hey! Do you see what I see?" And he pointed at a trail of footprints that their own had partly obliterated. "He's been here recently. Now what would he have to say to the Martians?"

"He?" said Mr. Boomschmidt. "Who? That's nothing. Lots of people come out here to get a look at real live Martians."

"Yeah, I suppose so," Freddy said. "But those footprints—you see the kind of herringbone sole and the triangle on the heel? Those are Anderson's prints."

"Well, Anderson's human, ain't he? That

means he's curious. What's strange about his coming up to have a look?"

"He was watching them play ball when I came," said Freddy. "Then he went down to the bank with me. But then *after* that he came back to the door of their wagon."

"Might have been before, not after, he went to the bank."

"No." Freddy had followed the tracks back a little way. "Because they're on top of these elephant tracks. And the elephant tracks were made when I first looked out your window and saw the Martians playing." He thought a minute. "And here's another thing that may be significant," he said. "Squeak-squeak is the only one who can't seem to learn English. Was that why he was kidnapped?"

Mr. Boomschmidt shook his head. "Good gracious, I don't know, Freddy. I'm completely puzzled."

Freddy was, too, but of course he didn't say so. "Well," he said, "I'd better go talk to Leo."

CHAPTER
5

The lion lived alone in a small trailer. When Freddy tapped on the door and was told to come in, he found Leo building a fire in the little wood stove. Leo shut the stove door and dusted off his paws. "Well, well, here's old woolly face! Ha! Take off your hat and coat and whiskers and sit down."

"Thankee," said Freddy. "I'll keep 'em on. Just want to find out where you stand on this baseball business. Your boss has hired me as coach, and he says you play after a fashion. What position?"

"I was captain," said Leo.

Freddy nodded his head. "Captain. Yeah. I can see that team now. Nine players and a captain. Look, lion," he said sharply. "The captain has to play, doesn't he? He can't just sit around and admire his pink fingernails. What did you play—shortstop, center field—"

"I caught," said Leo.

"Mice?" Freddy asked.

A deep rumbling growl came out of the lion's throat, and he walked stiff-legged toward his visitor. "Mister," he said, "that's the last straw!" He put a big paw on Freddy's shoulder. "I won't hurt you—not much. But I'm going to take you out and wash your face in the snow."

"In that case," said Freddy, in his natural voice, "I'd better take off my glasses." And he did so.

Leo stared at him, and slowly his nose wrinkled up in an expression of disgust. "Well, dye my hair!" he said. "You know, all the time there was something familiar about you. Not your face—there never is about that—even when you're not in disguise. But what's this all about? You're not really serious about this coaching job?"

"Sure. With Herc's help, and yours. And I'll get a book on it. Anyway, it's just an excuse to hang around and see what I can find out about Squeak-squeak." And he told Leo the story.

The lion knew that Squeak-squeak had disappeared, and that Freddy had been sent for. But he hadn't known that the Martians had changed their minds and refused help. He had no explanation for that. "What does the chief think?" he asked.

"I guess he thinks as I do," said Freddy, "that the Martians are in trouble, but that since they won't tell, all we can do is watch. And keep an eye on Anderson, because he's in it somewhere."

Leo stoked up the fire and made some cocoa. Freddy immediately spilled some on his beard, which had to be taken out in the kitchen and washed and then hung up to dry while they talked. Later, Freddy had supper at the Boomschmidts', and that evening the Martians and Leo and Oscar and Mr. Hercules came in to plan the baseball team.

Freddy thought they should begin practice

immediately, but Leo said: "You can't begin training in the winter. Spring's the time for that."

"We'll have to work indoors mostly," said Freddy. "And it won't accomplish much. But I figure that it will be awful good advertising. We'll put it in the paper that it's the sissy teams that go south for their spring training. We don't mind a little cold. We're tough and rugged. Hardened by winter training. All that stuff. And we'll have songs about it." He began to sing.

"The Martians are comin', Oho! Oho!
The Martians are comin', in mud, in snow.
   With bats and with balls and with fifes and
     with drummin',
The Martians are comin', Oho! Oho!

The Martians are comin', Hooray! Hooray!
The Dodgers and Yankees they'll play, they'll
     play!
   They'll mop up the earth, then they'll tackle
     the planets,
Constantly yellin' Hooray! Hooray!"

Oscar interrupted. "What vile doggerel!" he muttered. He was sitting in a corner with his legs folded under him, and he looked down his beak at Freddy with his big foolish eyes and

"Dad rat ye!" he said furiously.

said snippily: "Mr. Boom, is this shabby old person really to be our coach?" For of course Freddy still had on his disguise.

An ostrich has a kick like a mule, but he can't use it sitting down, and Mr. Boomschmidt's ceiling was so low that Oscar couldn't stand up straight enough to kick. He was cranky and stuck-up, even for an ostrich, and Freddy knew he would have trouble with him. He thought he might as well get it over. He got up and went across the room and slapped the big bird twice across the beak.

"Dad rat ye!" he said furiously. "Get out of here!" He tugged angrily at his beard. "Go on— git! You ain't going to be on any team I coach."

The slaps had hurt Freddy a lot worse than they had hurt Oscar, but Oscar didn't know that. He couldn't kick, so he hunched as far away from Freddy as he could. "You big bully! You wouldn't dare do that if we were outside!" he said.

"Probably not," Freddy said. "But we ain't outside, and I ain't going to have anything to do with ye outside. Git!"

"Well, I *must* say, you take a great deal upon yourself—" said Oscar "—ordering me out of Mr. Boom's house! Really, Mr. Boom, I think this person should leave instead of I."

"Me," said Mr. Boomschmidt.

"You?" said Oscar. "Certainly you should not—"

"No, no, *no*, Oscar!" Mr. Boomschmidt interrupted. "You said 'instead of I,' and you should have said 'instead of me.' "

"Instead of *you*?" Oscar was puzzled. "But why should I have said that? Nobody suggested that *you* leave."

"Goodness me, of course not," Mr. Boomschmidt said. "But you said—"

"Excuse me, chief," put in Leo, "but I'm getting kind of dizzy. If somebody's got to leave, suppose I go. I need air."

"Yuh, thut's right, 'Restes," said Mr. Hercules in his heavy voice. "Uh dunno what yuh talkin' about."

"Well, skip it then," said Mr. Boomschmidt, though it was plain that he was reluctant to stop trying to confuse everybody. "And let's come back to Mr. Arquebus. He's the boss of the team, Oscar. If he says you can't play, why my gracious, I guess you can't."

Oscar had been looking faintly cross-eyed with the effort to sort out "I" and "me" and find out what he had said wrong. He hadn't much brain and what he had was easily confused, so nobody was much surprised when he said: "But he promised I could play!"

"You can," Freddy said. "But if you do, you

ain't going to give me any of your sass. And you're going to obey orders. If you don't I'll get rid of you so quick you'll be going out the gate before you know you're fired."

Oscar sniffed, but obviously it was just a sort of general sniff and not directed at Freddy. Ostriches sniff a good deal, just to show how superior they would like to be to everybody else. If they were really superior, they wouldn't sniff. They wouldn't have to.

Mr. Hercules had got the Martians interested in baseball, but he wasn't very good at explaining, and—perhaps because he had bragged a good deal—they had got the impression that the purpose of the game was for the pitcher to hit the batter and knock him cold. If he did so, he scored one. If the batter could dodge and hit the ball, and knock the cover off it, that scored one for his side. It didn't sound like much of a game, even to Martians, whose national game is a simplified form of duck-on-a-rock. But when Freddy explained how baseball really worked, they became enthusiastic.

So after they had talked awhile, Freddy went back to Mrs. Peppercorn's to sleep. And the next morning they all got out for practice. It was clear and cold. Mr. Hercules and the Martians didn't mind, but Leo had on a red sweater the color of which clashed horribly with his beautifully curled orange-colored mane. Oscar had the arms of an old sweater cut off and pulled over his ankles. He complained a good deal, but when Mr. Boomschmidt, who was batting out fungoes, sent a few fast grounders his way, he picked them up and snapped them back with a queer underhand swing of his big claw.

The Martians, who had had some practice, were fairly good, too. They dashed around, squeaking and clicking happily. They usually caught with three hands, and when they ran for one, they dropped onto all fours—or all sixes— and looked more than ever like spiders on the thin carpet of white snow. Their hitting was bad, even for beginners, for they swung at every pitch. They seemed to think that that was the way to play. But Freddy didn't stop them, and he warned the others not to try to correct them. "I *want* them to think that's the way to play. Anyone that tells them different gets fired straight off the team."

Mr. Hercules was pretty good, but the first ball he threw back came so fast that it whistled like a bullet, and Mr. Boomschmidt made no effort to stop it, but threw himself flat on the ground. "Good gracious, Herc," he called as he got up and brushed himself off, "you tired of seeing me around? Toss 'em, will you." After that Mr. Hercules was more careful.

After they'd done this for a while, Freddy swept off the pitcher's mound and the home plate, and they all tried out for pitcher, while Leo caught. The best of the Martians was Chirp-squeak. He was the smallest and he didn't have much speed, but his control was better, and he could throw with all four arms. The first pitch would be upper left-handed, and the next one lower right-handed, and then He'd shift to one of the other two. Mr. Hercules had a terrifically fast ball, but his control wasn't very good, and later, when they took turns at bat, none of the batters would stand within three feet of the plate for fear of being hit. Leo, who said his big paws were tough enough to catch anything, finally had to use a mitt.

They practiced all morning, and came out again for a while in the afternoon. Then Freddy said: "I think we've had enough for today. Tomorrow I'll see if we can't get some of the boys from the school to give us a game. We can make up two partial teams, anyway. Because the way to learn to play ball is to play."

But the next day came a thaw. The snow melted, and though it was warm, the ground was soggy. Freddy said they ought to play anyway. He said that the harder the conditions were under which they learned to play, the better players they would be in the end. "If we can learn to play in the snow, and in the mud, just think how good we'll be when we have a good dry field to play on." But when he telephoned Mr. Finnerty at the high school, the coach just laughed at him. "Kind of rushing the season, aren't you, Mr. Arquebus?" he said. "Wait till spring. Then my boys'll give you a game. And by the way, you hadn't ought to play out there anyway—you'll cut the field all up and ruin it."

Freddy thought that made sense, so he telephoned Mr. Bean—still in the character of Mr. Arquebus, the circus coach—and asked him to let them have one of his fields to practice in. "We'll cut it up pretty bad," he said, "but I know you expect to plow that field anyway in the spring, and maybe when we get through with it you won't need to." So Mr. Bean thought that was a good idea and said yes.

CHAPTER

The Beans not only lent the ballplayers a field to practice in, but they offered them the hospitality of the farm for as long as they cared to stay. But only Leo, and Hannibal, the elephant, availed themselves of the offer. Oscar remarked snippily that he did not care to associate with vulgar farm animals, and came out on foot every day. "Likes to have folks stare at him," Leo said. "He makes a regular parade of it." Mr. Boomschmidt had to stay with the circus, and he and Mr. Hercules drove out every day, as did the Martians in their flying saucer.

The situation was more difficult for Freddy. But by appearing as himself most of the time, and in disguise only when on the ball field, and by giving out that Mr. Arquebus had rented a room in the pig pen, he got away with his double personality. Nobody noticed that Mr. Arquebus and Freddy were never both visible at the same time, or that often when one went into the pig pen, presently the other came out. And if the Beans recognized that old Prince Albert coat, they didn't say anything.

Now that the skating was gone, the farm animals didn't have much to do, and they came up and hung around and watched the baseball practice, and made cracks about the players. There were plenty of chances for that, for although the field was high, it dried off slowly, and the players churned it into mud two inches deep. The Martians ran over this lightly, and Hannibal was so big that he didn't notice it, but it was the middle-sized players—Leo and Mr. Boomschmidt and Mr. Hercules—who slipped

They were so plastered with mud that you couldn't tell a man from a lion.

and slithered and occasionally fell down, until they were so plastered with mud that you couldn't tell man from lion.

Jinx, who was probably Freddy's closest friend, and Mrs. Wiggins, who was his partner in the detective business, were the only farm animals that knew who Mr. Arquebus was. When in disguise, Freddy kept away from the others. At first, when he wasn't in disguise, they asked him a great many questions about the coach. Freddy had to make up some very fantastic explanations. He said Mr. Arquebus was a very old friend of Mr. Boomschmidt's, and had been almost as famous in baseball as Connie Mack. He said Mr. Arquebus believed that winter and early spring training in the North was the best way to harden his players. Of course as he was too old to play himself, he wore the whiskers to keep his face warm.

"Does he shave 'em off in summer?" Georgie asked.

"No, in summer they protect him from sunburn."

Finally the farm animals just accepted him, as the Martians and the circus animals had.

Freddy kept his room at Mrs. Peppercorn's, and on rainy days he stayed in Centerboro to keep an eye on Mr. Anderson. It was handy having the flying saucer nearly always available, with Two-clicks ready to fly him down. Mr. Anderson called several times at Mrs. Peppercorn's to see "my dear friend, Mr. Arquebus," as he called him. They talked about investments, but although Mr. Anderson didn't again try to persuade Mr. Arquebus to buy one of the houses he had for sale, Freddy felt that he was working up to a proposition of some kind.

Along about the first of April Mr. J. J. Pomeroy and his family came back from the South. Mr. Pomeroy was a robin, and the head of the A.B.I.: the Animal Bureau of Investigation. Freddy put him to work at once on "what I call," Freddy said, "the Case of the Vanishing Martian." He always gave a name like the title of a mystery story to any case he wanted Mr. Pomeroy to work on, because then the robin felt that his work was more important. And Freddy always said that people do their best work if they think what they're doing is important.

"The main thing is to watch the Martians," Freddy told him. "They claim they know where Squeak-squeak is, and that he's all right. Then why don't they tell me? And why are they so worried that they have to call me off the case? And why did Anderson go to see them? I want answers to those questions."

"You shall have them, sir; you shall have

them," said Mr. Pomeroy impressively, emphasizing his promise by taking off his spectacles with one claw and tapping them on the branch on which he was perched. "I will turn my whole staff to work on the case at once."

From any other robin this would have sounded very silly indeed. But Mr. Pomeroy, in spite of his pompousness, was a hard worker; he had organized his bureau with great care; and his staff was one which J. Edgar Hoover himself might have envied. For clever as an F.B.I. man may be, he cannot hide under a pieplant leaf like a rabbit; he cannot sit on a window sill and listen to a conversation without being noticed, like a bumblebee; nor can he, without being observed, shadow a suspect by sitting on the rim of his hat as a ladybug can. And these were only a few among the birds and animals and insects who had pledged loyalty to Mr. Pomeroy and the A.B.I.

The morning after Mr. Pomeroy came back, a large limousine drove into the barnyard and pulled up by the pig pen. The chauffeur got out and tapped on the door. "Good morning, Mr. Frederick," he said, as Freddy opened the door. "Mrs. Winfield Church to see you."

Freddy went out to the car. "Good morning, Mrs. Church," he said. "Will you excuse me if I don't ask you in? I have a house guest—Mr.

Arquebus, the baseball coach, and he isn't up yet."

"Don't blame him," said Mrs. Church. "Wouldn't be up myself if I didn't have to be. I'm in trouble, Freddy. Can you come out to the house with me?"

Freddy said of course, and indeed there was nothing he would not have done for Mrs. Church. For although she was rich and had a big red stone house in the upper part of town with turrets sticking up all over it, she was very fond of Mrs. Wiggins, and often drove out to the farm and took the cow for a ride, and to tea at some expensive restaurant. Indeed, she said that Mrs. Wiggins seemed more like a sister to her than her own sister, who lived in Scranton and never even sent her a Christmas card. She was fond of Freddy, too, and had been a help to him in several of his cases.

It had turned cold and snowed in the night, and the ground was white. Around the Church house the surface was unbroken except for Mrs. Church's footprints, coming down the front steps to where she had got in her car. "And I want you to notice that particularly, Freddy," she said. "No one has been in or out of this house since it stopped snowing, at ten o'clock last night.

"And yet," she said when they were inside

and were seated in the drawing room, "*Some-*body besides me was in the house last night. For look at this." She showed him a flat, leather-covered case about eight inches square, and snapped it open. It was empty.

"I wore my diamond necklace to the Methodist Church supper last night. When I got home, I put it in this case and left it on the dresser in the front room. This morning it was gone.

"Where did it go, Freddy? No one has been in or out of this house except me since ten last night. If a thief came in before ten, how did he get out?"

"Maybe he's still here," said Freddy. "Maybe he saw the snow and realized he couldn't escape until it melted, without leaving footprints."

Mrs. Church got up quickly. "Good gracious, I never thought of that," she said. "We must search the house."

"Er—just a minute," said Freddy, who wasn't specially anxious to go poking around in closets for a robber who was probably armed to the teeth. "It doesn't have to be a thief. Suppose a mouse dragged it off down a mouse hole. Suppose a—a crow flew in a window and carried it off. They like bright things."

"If your crow flew in my open window last night it couldn't get into the guest room because my door was closed. And how did your mouse open the case? Well, if you haven't any more animals to suggest, suppose we go look."

Freddy followed her reluctantly into the hall. She went into a closet and brought out a very rusty double-barreled shotgun.

"Is it loaded?" Freddy asked.

"Goodness, I don't know," said Mrs. Church. "How do you find out?"

Freddy broke open the breech. There were two shells in the chambers. He snapped the gun shut, shouldered it, and they set out.

"Well," said Freddy an hour later, "unless he went up the chimney I don't see how he got away. I've looked out of every window, and the snow isn't disturbed anywhere except on the roof under that unlocked window in the turret overlooking the garden—did you notice?—something seems to have pressed the snow down; it even seems to have rubbed some of the red paint off the roof. But it's four or five feet below the window."

"A branch might have fallen there during the night," Mrs. Church suggested. "But I didn't see any."

"I don't see how it can have anything to do with the necklace," Freddy said. "There'd have to be tracks leading up to it. And there aren't any."

Back in the drawing room they just looked at each other for a while without saying anything. Then Mrs. Church said suddenly: "Freddy, do you believe in ghosts?"

"Well," said Freddy thoughtfully, "I do and I don't, if you know what I mean."

"I know just what you mean," she said. "You do if they're there, and you don't if they're not there. Well, they've been here for the last few nights. You know I let all my servants go two years ago. I got tired of eating a big dinner at seven o'clock just because the cook thought I ought to, when maybe all I wanted was a hot dog and a coke at five. I got sick of asking people to do things for me that I could do myself in a quarter of the time. And what if the house *is* dusty? I like it that way." She lowered her voice. "And Freddy, twice last week I never made my bed at all!

"But about this ghost. You know, Freddy, if he'd stomp around and rattle chains and yell, I wouldn't mind him so much. But he's a quiet ghost. You just hear a kind of faint swish-swish out in the hall, and then he snuffles at the door. And then he'll sort of blow under the door, the way a dog does. I tell you, being alone in the house, it's pretty awful."

"How long has he been around?" Freddy asked.

"Oh, I guess about a week. But he's never touched any jewelry before. My goodness, I'd have given him the necklace if he'd asked for it, just to have him go away. Because it's either him or me. One of us has got to leave this house. I can't sit up night after night, shivering and shaking; why I've lost ten pounds already. Not that I don't need to lose it, but how do I know that he'll go away when I get down to the weight I ought to be?"

Freddy said: "And is it the ghost or the necklace you want me to try to do something about?"

Mrs. Church laughed. "You guessed it, Freddy. It's the ghost. Just between you and me, that necklace came from the five and ten. I sold all my real jewelry years ago. Why wear real jewels when for twenty-five cents you can get just as much sparkle out of glass? No, what I'd really like you to do is catch this ghost for me."

Freddy said: "I don't seem to want to very much, Mrs. Church."

"Really?" she said. "Have you ever spent a night in a haunted house? I should think it would be most interesting."

"If it *is* a ghost," Freddy said, "I don't see what I could do about it. On the other hand, if it's something else, maybe I can. Now as I just said, I don't believe in the ghost, because he's not here now. And as long as I don't believe in him, I can believe all the snuffling and swishing is something else, and maybe I can do something about it. But if I should hear him, then I'd believe in him, and I wouldn't be any use."

"All right, all right," said Mrs. Church impatiently. "I suppose that's one way of getting out of it. Though after all, what can a ghost do to you? Moan and groan and make faces—that's all. If it was a real burglar, I wouldn't think of asking you to try to help catch him. But—"

"Excuse me, Mrs. Church," Freddy said. "Let me tell you about the last time I tried to catch a ghost. That ghost was Mr. Anderson, the real estate man. He had false faces and luminous paint, and a bunch of rats to help him, and he was haunting the Lakeside Hotel. A Mrs. Fillmore owned it, and he thought he could drive her out and buy it cheap. Well, we caught him, and we made him sign a confession, too. But every time I hear of a house being haunted, I wonder if Mr. Anderson is trying to buy it cheap.

"I don't say it's Anderson. He couldn't have got in here without leaving tracks. And there aren't any rats. But it just makes me suspicious. Let me ask you to do this: offer a reward for the return of the necklace, and let's see what happens."

"But it only cost twenty-five cents," said Mrs. Church.

"All right. Put it in the paper like this: One-third of the value of the necklace stolen from me last Tuesday night will be paid for its return and no questions asked."

Mrs. Church laughed. "Freddy, you kill me!" she said. "Won't they be surprised when I pay them eight and a third cents!" Then she stopped. "But Freddy, nobody could have stolen it. I mean, no human. They just couldn't! You didn't hear that thing snuffling around my door! Freddy, you can bring anybody you want to with you, but if you won't stay here tonight, I'm moving out. I won't spend another night like last night."

Freddy hesitated. Mrs. Church had never appealed to him for help before. Even now she didn't remind him of the times when she had helped him. The thought of sitting in that dark upper room, waiting for some supernatural monster to come slithering down the hall, snuffling greedily at the door, made his tail come completely uncurled. But this was his friend. She needed his help.

"All right," he said. "I'll do it."

CHAPTER
7

A month ago Freddy had ordered a special large-sized catcher's mask for Leo. The regular mask the lion had been wearing was much too small for his face; it looked like a mouse trap perched on his nose, and when it slipped sideways, as it sometimes did, it just covered one eye. When Mrs. Church drove Freddy home he wanted to stop in the sporting-goods department of the Busy Bee and see if the mask had come. But when they drove down Main Street, there didn't seem to be a parking space for blocks, and Freddy said never mind, he'd get it later.

But Mrs. Church laughed. "Riley will find us a parking space," she said. And sure enough just beyond the Busy Bee, the chauffeur swung the car in over the curb and right into a store whose doorway had been widened to admit it. "I do a lot of shopping at the Busy Bee," she explained. "But I don't like to walk, so I bought this store and had it altered to park in. I suppose some people would think it was extravagant," she said. "But it's a lot more useful than a diamond necklace."

Freddy picked up the mask and they drove out to the farm. Mrs. Church wanted to call on Mrs. Wiggins, so she went into the cow barn. The flying saucer was parked with a number of Centerboro cars at one side of the barnyard, and looking up toward the practice field, Freddy could see a row of spectators leaning on the fence, among them Mr. Anderson, and the Centerboro High coach, Mr. Finnerty. He went up to the pig pen and got into his disguise, and then went over to the field.

Today two eight-man teams were playing a

regular game. Jason Brewer and Henry James and two other boys had come out from Centerboro, and Jimmy Witherspoon had come down through the Big Woods and picked up Peter, the bear, and Mac, the wildcat, on his way. Peter was pitching. Like most bears, he pitched underhand. He had just, much to his surprise, struck out Mr. Hercules. Two-clicks stepped up. The first pitch was over the plate, but too low. The Martian let it go by and Mr. Bean, who was umpiring, called a ball.

Freddy frowned and tugged at his beard. He watched the second pitch. The Martian swung at it and Freddy's face cleared. But he walked over to Chirp-squeak, who was on deck. "Will you boys please remember what I told you!" he said sharply. "We've got company today." He indicated the row of spectators.

Chirp-squeak replied that he and the other Martians had got to wondering and they thought it would be better to let the very high ones go by.

"Look," said Freddy, "when we have company I want you to go right on swinging at everything. No matter where the pitch comes, swing at it! I don't care if you strike out."

But even when they picked 'em, they didn't hit very well, any of them, said the Martian. "You like we throw this games?"

"I want you to do as you're told," Freddy said angrily. "I don't care if you lose this game. I don't care if you lose to Centerboro High, later on. I want you to win your important games, and if you do as I say, you will."

Chirp-squeak grumbled a little, but five minutes later, when he had waved his bat ineffectively at three wild pitches and returned to the bench, Freddy heard him mutter: "I hope you satisfy, you big ape!"

"Dear me," said Mr. Boomschmidt, who had overheard the remark, "how quickly these Martians are picking up our good homely American talk, now that they've begun to play baseball! Really a fine thing for them."

"Yeah," said Freddy. "They sure are learning a fine American disrespect for anyone in authority."

Mr. Boomschmidt lowered his voice. "Why do you let 'em swing at everything the way they do? You can't teach 'em to hit that way."

"Don't you know why?" Freddy asked.

"No," said Mr. Boomschmidt. "No, I can't say I— Oh, my goodness!" he said suddenly. "Is it . . . ?"

"Don't say it," Freddy cut in. "Maybe it's kind of tricky, but I think it's fair. Particularly when we play the Tushville town team. Because they won all their games last year, but they didn't win fair and square. I'm pretty sure that pitcher, John Smith, was a professional. Judge Willey thought he looked an awful lot like Lefty Zingwall, who used to pitch for Rochester. And there were two others that certainly weren't amateurs, either."

"Tcha!" said Mr. Boomschmidt disgustedly. "Pretty poor sports. Why do you have to play them?"

"We don't, of course. But Kurtz, their manager—he's been over watching our practice—he's up there now, next to Mr. Anderson—see him?—he wrote asking for a game or two. I don't like Kurtz, or Tushville either, much, and I think we can lick them. And—well, I've been puzzling how we were going to get uniforms. You know ready-made uniforms won't fit this team. Look at 'em—an elephant, a lion, four Martians with four arms each—well, you see what I mean. It will cost a fortune."

"Goodness, I see what you mean," said Mr. Boomschmidt. "But think what a crowd a team from Mars will bring out—at fifty cents a head. Or have you thought of that? Of course, I see you have. My gracious, Freddy, are you really as smart as that, or do I just think so because you have that long white beard on?"

At that moment a wasp lit on Freddy's hat brim, walked down under it, and disappeared in

A wasp lit on Freddy.

his beard just in front of his ear. Freddy shivered. There was a wasp named Jacob who was a good friend of his, and one of the cleverest operatives in the A.B.I.; but it is hard to tell one wasp from another, and suppose this was a stranger! "Hey!" he said. "Come out of there, will you?"

"Keep your whiskers on, pig," said Jacob's sharp little voice. "This is Agent W-2 reporting for Chief Pomeroy. Wanna see my credentials?" He crawled up through the whiskers and waved his sting close to Freddy's eye.

"Hey, go on and make your report and quit that funny business," Freddy growled. He knew of Jacob's fondness for practical jokes, and that they were sometimes painful.

"O.K., kid, here it is," said the wasp. "Report on Martians. Nothing suspicious observed. No connection with Mr. Anderson noted. Subjects leave home every morning in flying saucer, arrive one minute later at Bean farm; practice baseball until five thirty, then return in saucer to Centerboro. Twice, at ten P.M., subjects have left in saucer for parts unknown, returning about 2 A.M. Impossible to tail saucer, whose speed faster than that of any known bug, bird, or insect. Impossible to report conversations, as we have no operatives who speak Martian.

"Report on E. H. Anderson. Normal activity connected with business during day. Spends part of afternoons at Bean farm watching practice. Had dinner last two evenings at Dixon's Diner, came home, stopping both times on way to buy large bag of peanuts, read until 10 P.M. when went upstairs. Light in bedroom out at 10.10. End of report.

"The chief wants to know," Jacob added, "if there are any further instructions, or do we keep on as before?"

"And you're absolutely certain that Anderson wasn't out of the house last evening?" Freddy asked.

"We had an operative on the roof of his porch, right under his bedroom window, all night, and another stationed on the garbage-can cover on the back porch."

"O.K.," said Freddy. "Keep a close watch tonight. Now you'd better buzz off." So Jacob did.

"Funny," Freddy said to Mrs. Wiggins later. "I'd have sworn Anderson was up to his old tricks, haunting Mrs. Church's house. But it can't be him."

"Don't see why it has to be," the cow replied. "Centerboro is certainly big enough to support more than one ghost. Good grief, Freddy, maybe it's a real ghost!"

"I never heard of a ghost that stole jewelry, before," said the pig. He tugged perplexedly at his beard.

"You've got to stop that yanking at your whiskers," said the cow. "You do it when you're disturbed about something, and sometime you're going to pull 'em right off and make a monkey of Mr. Arquebus."

"Make a pig of him," said Freddy. "O.K., I'll be careful."

"Maybe you ought to wear that outfit tonight," said Mrs. Wiggins. "I'd like to see that ghost when he opens the door and sees you. You'll scare him out of seven years' growth."

"He'll scare me out of eight if he does open it," Freddy said worriedly. "Look, Mrs. W., why not come along?"

But the cow said no thanks, she'd prefer to take her ghosts second-hand. And why didn't Freddy take Jinx?

So Freddy went off to talk to Jinx about it.

CHAPTER

8

At ten o'clock that night Freddy and Jinx were sitting in Mrs. Church's bedroom, in the dark, waiting for the ghost. Mrs. Church had locked herself into the guest room. They had searched the house carefully and Jinx said he'd bet his collection of catnip mice to a saucer of sour milk that there was nothing alive in it bigger than a spider. In addition, Mr. Pomeroy had arranged to have the grounds patrolled all night by two of his most capable operatives, Rabbits No. 12 and No. 23, who would give the alarm if they saw anyone trying to get in.

Freddy, also, had made elaborate preparations for the ghost's reception. If it came snuffling under the bedroom door tonight it would get one or two unpleasant surprises.

The first hour passed peacefully. Jinx curled up luxuriously in the middle of the bed. It wasn't often that he had a chance to lie around on a clean counterpane. If he tried it at home, Mrs. Bean chased him out with a broom. Freddy amused himself by making up a poem. Under his breath he recited the first lines to Jinx.

> *"It strikes me—does it not strike you?—*
> *That the average pig has a high I.Q."*

Jinx raised his head from his paws. He whispered crossly:

> *"It strikes me, and it strikes me hard,*
> *That the pig is a big fat hunk of lard."*

Then he dropped his head and closed his eyes again.

Freddy grinned and started another poem.

"The house is dark, the house is still,
And the black bat sits on the window sill.

Silent he sits till the midnight hour
And his little red eyes, they glimmer and
  glower."

"And then he goes in and takes a shower,"
said Jinx. "Shut up, Freddy, will you? I want
to sleep."
But Freddy went on.

"Slinking and slithering down the hall
The old gray ghost comes hugging the wall;

He tries the knobs of each of the doors,
And listens to hear if anyone snores.

And if he thinks that somebody's in
He gives a perfectly awful grin,

And licks his chops, and stoops to the floor,
And snuffles and whuffles under the door.

And the black bat on the window sill,
He wakes, and he cheeps both loud and shrill.

He cheepeth once, he cheepeth twice,
He cheepeth three times three;

And the ghost in the hall he begins to crawl;
Under the door he squeezes small;

And the—"

"Oh, shut *up,* Freddy!" Jinx whispered. "What are you trying to do—scare me?"

"I—I guess I've scared myself," said the pig. "I don't know why it is that times like this I don't really get scared until I begin to think I ought to be. And then I try to scare myself. I guess I can scare myself worse than any old ghost can."

At that moment there *was* a snuffling and whuffling under the door.

"Ugh!" said Freddy, as his tail came completely uncurled. "No I can't either." But he had to carry out his plan, no matter how scared he was. He tiptoed over to the bed and whispered: "Are you ready? Stand by with the pepper when I open the door."

But there was no answer. And the whuffling under the door grew louder.

"Jinx!" Freddy whispered. He felt over the bed. No cat there. He felt farther, and way down under the covers against the footboard his bore-trotter touched a lump—a lump that squirmed and let out a screech of pure terror.

The screech was muffled under the clothes, but it must have startled the ghost, for he stopped whuffling.

Freddy realized that he could expect no help from Jinx. He picked up the teacup, which he had filled with black pepper, and went to the door. Without pausing a second—for he knew if he did he would never again get up courage to turn that key—he unlocked the door, flung it open, and threw the pepper full in the face of the dim figure he saw kneeling before the threshold.

"Tchaa!" said the ghost, and then exploded in a series of the most terrific sneezes. "Ah-a-achaa! Choof! Hup, hup, hup—CHOW!" But he managed to get up and to stumble in blind haste down the hall toward the front stairs.

Freddy had been prepared for that. "Mrs. Church!" he called, and Mrs. Church, who had been waiting behind the guest-room door, came running out. She followed him to the head of the stairs.

The ghost, coughing and sneezing and reeling from side to side of the stairway, was half-way down. Now Freddy had taken all the tacks out of the stair carpet before locking himself into the room. So when he said: "Catch hold!" and they both bent and took hold of the top end of the carpet; and then said: "Pull!" and they

They both gave a strong yank.

both gave a strong yank—the carpet just straightened out and began moving upward under the feet of the ghost. Even the most weightless of ghosts could not have kept his footing on such a moving inclined plane, and Freddy judged, by the sound of the first bump as he hit the stairs, that he must weigh well over two hundred. The succeeding bumps were no gentler, and ended with a slow cartwheel, at the end of which the ghost lay for a moment flat on his face in the lower hall.

"Remarkable performance," said Mrs. Church. "Wish we'd had more light so we could have really seen it."

Freddy had hoped to get downstairs and tie the ghost up while he was helpless, but it was slow work getting down over that loose carpet. Finally they had to pull it up before they could walk down the bare stairs. And by that time the ghost had picked himself up and stumbled off to safety through the kitchen and the back door. And all they could see was that he had a black mask on. Neither of them could swear that he was Mr. Anderson. Freddy said angrily: "I could have caught him if I'd had the sense to slide down the banisters. What's the matter with me, anyway?"

"Just the same," said Mrs. Church, "I don't believe he'll try this business again. We know he isn't a real ghost, and he knows we know it. I'll just let it be known that, whoever he is, he can expect a charge of buckshot next time he comes. Now come on out in the kitchen. There's a gallon of ice cream in the refrigerator. Where's Jinx?"

He appeared just as they were taking their first bite. "H'm," he said jauntily, "I thought I heard dishes rattling. Well, what happened?"

"Yeah, what happened!" said Freddy scornfully. "What happened to you? Crawling down under the covers like a coward. A lot of help you were!"

"Oh now, Freddy," Jinx protested. "You know, that whooshing sound—I could have sworn that came from the foot of the bed. Sure I was under the covers—that's where the sound came from. I went for that ghost just like you said we ought to. Teeth and claws, Freddy—teeth and claws; didn't you hear me give the old war cry? Well, I suppose you couldn't, when I was under that blanket. Almost got him, too. He slugged me, and then I grabbed for him but he wasn't there. Must have slipped out under the mattress somehow."

"Oh, sure," said Freddy. "He slugged you! That's when I touched you, and you let out a screech—golly, were you scared!"

"Scared!" Jinx was indignant. "Say look, pig,

any time you see this cat scare— Yow!" he yelled suddenly. "What's that!" And he gave one bound on to the mantelpiece. For something had tapped at the window.

Even Mrs. Church had to laugh when she looked around and saw the white face and big ears of a rabbit on the other side of the pane. She opened the window and he hopped in. He saluted Freddy and said: "No. 23 reporting. Large man just came out of front door, ran off toward Main Street, sneezing. May have hay fever, or be starting a cold. I did not follow him, as my instructions were to watch the house."

"Did you recognize him?" Freddy asked.

"No, sir. He had on a mask. I should perhaps add that neither No. 12 nor I saw him come into the house. That of course is what we were watching for."

Freddy dismissed the rabbit and said to Mrs. Church: "I guess we didn't get anywhere much. We may suspect that it was Anderson, but we don't know and can't prove it. And even if we could—well, how did he get into the house? Without being seen by the rabbits?"

"My gracious, Freddy," said Mrs. Church, "maybe he really is a ghost."

Freddy shook his head. "No," he said. "But I tell you how we can find out. You go to Anderson and tell him the house is haunted and you can't live there any more. I think what he says will tell us whether he's our ghost or not."

"I'll see him in the morning," said Mrs. Church. "Now, for goodness sake, eat up this ice cream. And you'll stay here tonight. I tell you I'll feel a lot safer with you two in the house, even if our ghost did fall downstairs with his nose full of pepper."

Jinx and Freddy spent the night in the big bed in the guest room. They had eaten so much ice cream that they had to pile on the blankets to get warm. Jinx had been rather quiet, but just as Freddy was dropping off to sleep the cat nudged him. "Hey look, Freddy," he said. "I—now—I wish you wouldn't say anything back home about—well, about—you know—tonight."

"You mean about how scared you were when you hid under the covers?"

"Oh now, Freddy! Maybe it was a mouse that I heard. That was it—a mouse! He got down in the bed somehow, and I heard him and went after him. That's why I didn't hear whoever it was at the door. Look, Freddy, you know I don't get scared easily. You know I'm—" He broke off as a deep humming noise sounded somewhere outside. It increased for a moment or two, then suddenly faded away and was gone.

"Hey!" Freddy exclaimed. "Did you hear that?"

But there was no reply, and when Freddy reached out to shake the cat's shoulder, thinking perhaps he had gone to sleep, no cat was there. He sat up and looked. At the foot of the bed there was a cat-sized lump under the bedclothes.

"Oh gosh," Freddy said, "another mouse! Well, all right, let him stay there. But what's that flying saucer doing around here at this time of night? I'll have to investigate that."

CHAPTER

9

The first thing in the morning Freddy put on his disguise and had Riley drive him out to the ball park. He went over to where the flying saucer was parked. He climbed up on the disk and tapped at the door in the turret. After a minute Two-clicks threw it open. The Martian seemed very sleepy; he kept rubbing his eyes, and the third eye wasn't even open yet.

"You boys were out pretty late last night," Freddy said. "I'm not holding you down to regular training rules, but if I were, you'd be in trouble if you were out after ten. But you were flying around at one this morning. That's too late."

Two-clicks opened his third eye and looked at the pig accusingly. "You spy on us," he said.

"No," said Freddy. "I heard you. What were you doing over on the south side of town?"

"Sometimes," the Martian replied in his squeaky English, "we no can sleep. Sometime maybe me, maybe Chirp-squeak, no sleep. Take saucer for little fly around. Earth air very thick. We fly up, up—get thin air. Like home. Then we sleep."

"Yeah?" Freddy said to himself. "That saucer wasn't up, up last night. It was down, down, right over the roof and not on the south side of town, either." But aloud he only said, "O.K. Well, don't be late today. Mr. Finnerty is bringing over a scratch team from the high school to play us this afternoon."

On the way, as Riley was driving him out to the farm, he stopped and bought a bag of peanuts, which he stuffed into the tail pocket of his coat. Jacob was waiting for him with his A.B.I. report. There was nothing very exciting in it. Mr. Anderson had followed the same routine as on previous evenings. The operatives had not seen him leave the house after returning from dinner at the diner. And no one but he had entered the house in the past twenty-four hours.

Up on the field there was still quite a lot of work to be done before the game that afternoon. The pitcher's mound had been built up and a square stone had been sunk in the ground for home plate. But the foul lines still had to be marked in white, and the bases, which Mrs. Bean had made of canvas and stuffed with hay, had to be fastened in place. The ground had dried out well, and by noon Freddy, with the help of Leo and Hannibal and some of the farm animals, had the diamond in pretty fair shape.

At two o'clock the boys from Centerboro High arrived. They were very much excited at the prospect of playing such an oddly assorted team, although by this time they were well acquainted with the Martians, as well as with Mr. Boomschmidt, Mr. Hercules, and the circus animals, many of whom had at various times been guests in their own homes. Freddy of course they knew, but not as Mr. Arquebus, and several of them had a hard time repressing their giggles when they were introduced to this queer old white-whiskered man and told he was the coach.

The game hadn't been advertised, but word of it had got out, and there were nearly a hundred spectators hanging on the fence when it began. Freddy didn't move around much for fear of bumping into people, but by lifting his glasses and taking a quick squint under them, he made out that among the watchers was Mr. Anderson, and beside him, in earnest conversation, Mr. Kurtz, manager of the Tushville town team.

The visitors came to bat first. Jason Brewer, pitcher for Centerboro High, led off. Chirp-squeak, with four arms, all of which he could throw with, and with seven fingers on each hand, which gave him an amazing number of ways of gripping and releasing the ball, had developed a variety of curves and drops. His famous "skip ball," which gave a sort of double bounce as it crossed the plate, has never been duplicated. His one fault was that he hadn't a really fast ball. However, his left-hand pitches were a little faster than the ones with his right hands, so that he managed to control some change of speed.

His first pitch was with his upper right, and Jason tipped it for a foul. But when he took the ball in his lower left hand and began his wind-up, Jason became puzzled, and just stood and watched the ball as it floated over the plate.

Jimmy Witherspoon, confused by the four-arm pitching, struck out with three wild swings.

"Str-r-r-ike!" Mr. Bean called. Then, thoroughly confused by a lower-left pitch, the boy swung wildly at a high ball, and was out.

Of the next two boys up, Henry James hit a high fly to left field, but Mr. Hercules caught in with one hand, and Jimmy Witherspoon, confused by the four-arm pitching, struck out with three wild swings.

Jason Brewer had a fast ball, and pretty good control, but the Martians, who had had some experience with Mr. Hercules's sizzling delivery, weren't afraid of it. Two-clicks fouled twice and then singled; Chirp-squeak fanned at the first two pitches, which were way outside, but connected with the third one for a two-bagger, and then Leo came up. To his disgust, the lion swung at the first pitch and knocked up a little pop fly that dropped softly into Jason's glove.

The next two up in batting order on the Martian team were Click-two-squeaks and Chirp. Freddy watched the former as he swung at the first three pitches—and struck out: one, two, three. He knew that Chirp would do the same. But that was all right. That was what he wanted them to do. He stumbled over to where Mr. Anderson and Mr. Kurtz were now chatting with Mr. Finnerty.

"Well, Mr. Arquebus," Mr. Finnerty said, "we're even so far. Why do you let your Martians bat like that? They swing at everything—good, bad, and indifferent. Have they had much batting practice?"

Freddy smoothed his long beard, behind which he was grinning happily. "Dad rat 'em!" he said irritably. "Can't seem to teach 'em to wait for the good ones. They seem to think they ain't playin' unless they're beatin' the air with them bats."

Freddy didn't see much through his glasses, but he did see Mr. Anderson turn to Mr. Kurtz and wink at him.

Mr. Finnerty shook his head. "Jason's getting onto that already," he said. "It's too bad; you've got some good baseball material there."

"Understand you and Boomschmidt want to get some local games before the circus starts on the road this summer," said Mr. Kurtz. "We've got a good little town team over at Tushville. They aren't big-league stuff—though some of 'em might be some day—but I guess they could give you some competition. How about it?"

"Well now, mister," Freddy said, "I ain't nothing but the coach; you'll have to talk to Boomschmidt. He owns the team." He pulled out his bag of peanuts and offered them to the three men. Mr. Finnerty and Mr. Kurtz each took a few, but Mr. Anderson shook his head. "Never touch 'em," he said.

There was a sharp crack, and Mr. Finnerty yelled: "Hey, look at that!" The ball was flying high over the second baseman's head, and Mr. Boomschmidt's little fat legs were twinkling past first. As he touched second, the right fielder reached for it—and missed. And Mr. Boomschmidt tore on past third and then home.

There was a burst of applause, which he acknowledged by taking off his hat and waving it at the crowd; then he came across to where Freddy was standing. "Good gracious, coach," he said, "how did I ever do that? A home run!" He laughed. "I'd better run home with my home run and tell Rose."

"You'd better stay here and knock another of those things; you're going to need it," said Mr. Finnerty. "Your pitcher has just struck out." And indeed Chirp-squeak had done what his two team-mates had done; he had struck at the first three balls pitched to him—and missed all three.

Nevertheless at the end of the second inning the score was one and one.

The rest of the game was like the first inning. The Martians struck out with rather tiresome regularity. Mr. Boomschmidt didn't get another hit, but Oscar and Hannibal got three hits apiece, and Mr. Hercules, who had been warned not to swing too hard, got a three-base hit and a homer. But the high-school boys began to get a little used to Chirp-squeak's quadruple delivery, and by the end of the ninth had piled up eight runs, to the Martians' six.

Freddy was well satisfied, however. And he was even more pleased when he walked up to where Mr. Kurtz and Mr. Boomschmidt were standing and heard the latter say: "Oh my goodness, oh my gracious, yes! We certainly should be able to charge a dollar admission. That ought to mean at least a thousand tickets. Well now, that's good money. How'll we divide the gate receipts? Even?"

"How about two-thirds to the winner?" said Mr. Kurtz. "Ought to be a little extra incentive to win. Not that I'm at all sure Tushville can beat you. You've got some tough competition there. But my boys will play better if they think there's a little money in winning."

"Well, I think that is O.K.," said Mr. Boomschmidt. "But I want to talk it over with the Martians first, naturally. My, my, what a game that'll be! We'll give 'em a good build-up in the newspapers—tell how the Martians are great baseball fans, and how they've sent their best team to earth to challenge our teams, and to try to get up an Interplanetary League. My, my, won't we make the World Series look like baby stuff!" He turned to Freddy. "Hear that,

Mr. Arquebus? S'pose you can get these boys in shape to play a couple games with Tushville around May 15th?"

"Play 'em tomorrow if you say so," Freddy replied. "This here Tushville team—I've heard about 'em. They ain't very hot stuff, but I guess it'll be good practice for the boys."

Through his glasses Freddy saw Mr. Kurtz's face turn from a pale blur to a pink one. "I made him mad," he thought.

But Mr. Kurtz only said mildly: "Why, that's so, I guess. My boys have only got two hands apiece and there ain't any of 'em can bat with his nose like that elephant. But it'll be good practice for them, too. Now where'll we have the first game—Centerboro or Tushville?"

"You'd better decide that, Mr. Boom," Freddy said, and turned away. He wanted to think. Mr. Kurtz was known to be hot-tempered; telling him his team wasn't much good had made him angry; then why had he given such a mild answer? And why had he practically agreed that Tushville couldn't win? Centerboro had just beaten the Martians, and the Tushville town team could certainly lick Centerboro High.

Suddenly Freddy laughed. It had come to him what Mr. Kurtz was up to. He wanted to pretend that his team wasn't any good so that he could coax Mr. Boom into letting the winner take the biggest part of the gate receipts. Well, that was all right, too. Certainly, judging by this game today, Tushville would have an easy win. But he had a trick up his sleeve for that.

CHAPTER
10

Freddy and Mr. Boomschmidt were well pleased with the outcome of the game, even though they had lost. When Mr. Finnerty suggested that the Martians play a few regular games with the high-school team, with charged admissions, on the town diamond, they agreed.

"But we ain't going to play you until we've cleaned up these Tushville sports," Freddy said. "They're our first official games."

"You know," Mr. Finnerty said, "I think maybe I can figure out why you want to get those Tushville games off the calendar before you play anybody else. I've been watching your practice closely, and while Kurtz may know the game pretty well, he hasn't been in baseball as long as I have. Or as long as you have, Mr. Arquebus. Well, I don't like that gang of Tushville rowdies. They haven't a high school team over there, so we don't even have to go there at all. We had trouble enough last year with one football game, so you can count on my keeping my mouth shut. But in the meantime, we can have a few unofficial games, can't we?"

"Anytime, mister; anytime," said Freddy.

"Well, well, Henry; congratulations!" said a voice behind him, and Mr. Anderson gave him a slap on the back that nearly knocked the wind out of him. "Your boys certainly put up a fine game. By the way," he said, lowering his voice, "how did you come out at the bank? Did they take care of you all right?"

"Oh, them?" said Freddy. "Stuck-up lot of critters, I thought 'em. No sir, they're too nosey. Asked more questions than you could shake a stick at. Why I wouldn't leave my money in that place no more'n I'd toss it in the gutter. No sir, it's where I know where it is, and it's going to stay there." And he tapped his breast pocket significantly.

"Very wise of you," said Mr. Anderson. "But I've got a little real estate proposition coming up—well, in a day or two I'll drop round. I promise you it'll interest you."

Early that evening, Freddy, having left his disguise in the pig pen, went to Centerboro to see Mrs. Church. He was just in time, she told him; Mr. Anderson had just telephoned and asked if he might come round in half an hour, he had something important to tell her. "What do you suppose he wants?" she said. "I haven't said anything yet about the house being haunted."

Freddy said he couldn't imagine.

There was a small closet or coatroom off the hall right outside the parlor. When the doorbell rang, Freddy went inside and pulled the door nearly shut. When Mrs. Church had taken Mr. Anderson into the parlor, he heard the latter say: "I suppose you're wondering why I wanted to see you, ma'am. Well, I'll come to the point right away. I was having my breakfast this morning when the phone rang, and a strange voice wanted to know if I'd seen your ad in the

Centerboro paper about the reward for the return of your necklace. I said yes, I was just
reading the paper.

" 'Well,' says this fellow, 'I've got that necklace, and I want you to act as go-between and
collect the reward. I'll give you a third.'

"Well, I laughed and said: 'Why pick on me?
Why not do it yourself?'

"So he said no, you'd get the police in on it
—set a trap for him. 'But I can trust you,' he
says. 'I know all about you,' he says. 'You're an
honest man, and you'll keep your mouth shut if
you promise to.'

"Well, I thought about you, ma'am, and how
if I didn't collect the reward for him, you'd
probably never see that necklace again. He'd
break it up and peddle the diamonds around
and get what he could for 'em. So I said: 'O.K.,
bring it over here right now.'

"Well, he brought it, and here it is." Freddy
could hear the click of the beads as they were
handed over. "Of course I don't want any part
of the reward. I'm glad to be of service."

"Who was the thief? What did he look
like?" Mrs. Church asked.

"I'm sorry; I gave my word not to say anything about that. He's waiting now for the reward, so if it's all right—"

"Of course," said Mrs. Church. "I'll get the

reward. But first, there's something I want to speak to you about. I intended to call you up this morning. It's this house. I— Well, it sounds very silly to say it in broad daylight, but it's haunted."

"Oh now, my dear Mrs. Church!" he protested. "Of course, as a real estate man, in the business for thirty years, I have run across two or three houses that were unquestionably haunted. One, I remember, was infested with ghouls—dreadful tall white creatures that glided about screeching and gnashing their teeth. Did you ever hear anyone gnash his teeth, Mrs. Church? A truly awful sound, and of course makes it quite impossible to sleep. And another house—there were giant spiders in the attic. They used to come down and race up and down the upper hall after dark, squeaking. That house, I remember, had to be burned. And yet— Are you quite *sure*, Mrs. Church, that what you may have seen and heard wasn't just, say, the wind, and a blowing curtain?"

So then Mrs. Church described the slithering and the whuffling outside her bedroom door, and Mr. Anderson kept saying: "Dear, dear!" and "Mercy gracious!" and when she had finished he said: "Well, ma'am, that does sound serious. But I don't quite see how I can be of help to you. Of course I'm glad to do anything I can—"

"You can sell the house for me. That's what I shall have to do. I got rid of my servants because they were more bother than they were worth—always in the way and giving me no privacy. But if I can't live in a house with servants, I certainly can't live with ghosts. At least the servants stayed in bed at night. What do you think this house would bring?"

"Well," said Mr. Anderson thoughtfully, "of course if it gets out that the place is haunted—"

"I won't conceal that fact," she said. "I'm not going to have the buyer come back and say that I sold him the house without telling him honestly what was wrong with it."

"Well, you have told me," said Mr. Anderson. "Suppose I buy it?"

"How much would you give?" she asked.

"I'll be frank with you, ma'am," he said. "I'd expect to resell it, and for that I'd have to find a family that didn't mind ghosts. Perhaps I couldn't, and then I'd be stuck with it. That house with the ghouls in it—I sold it to some people that thought it would be fun. They thought maybe one of the ghouls would make a fourth at bridge. But they only stayed there a week and I had to give their money back. Finally I sold it for a hundred dollars to a carpenter who tore it down for the lumber in it. And then the lumber was haunted. He built himself a back porch with some of it, and one ghoul sat out there every night and screamed."

"So you couldn't give me much for the house?" Mrs. Church said.

"I could only give you a fraction of what it's worth," he said, "and if you know anything about fractions—well, it won't be much. I'm sorry. If I were buying it for myself it would be different. I am not afraid of ghosts; in fact—"

At that moment Freddy, who was getting stiff and wanted to change his position slightly, got his feet entangled in some rubbers and overshoes on the floor of the closet. He grabbed at one of the coats that was hanging on a pole that ran lengthwise through the closet, and the coat came rustling down over his head, while the hanger fell with a rattle to the floor.

He froze as he heard Mr. Anderson say sharply: "What's that? I thought we were alone in the house."

"We are. What's the matter?" There was calm surprise in Mrs. Church's voice. Freddy heard Mr. Anderson get up. Quickly he draped the cloak which had fallen over him about his

He danced down the hall, the cloak trailing on the floor.

head and shoulders. It was a huge plum-colored cape with a hood.

"You didn't hear *that?*" Mr. Anderson demanded. He started for the hall.

"I didn't hear a thing," she asserted.

Freddy grasped what he felt was his only chance. "Now if she only pretends not to *see* anything," he thought. And as Mr. Anderson came out of the parlor door, the pig came with a sort of dancing step out of the closet. With his back to the gaping Mr. Anderson he danced down the hall, the cloak trailing on the floor behind him, and with a shrill squeal disappeared through the kitchen door.

The sight of this hooded and dancing dwarf and the sound of his inhuman squeals was too much for Mr. Anderson. He ran back into the parlor, slammed the door, and put his shoulder to it. "You saw!" he gasped. "You saw that—that creature!"

Mrs. Church came to the door. "What creature?" she asked. "What are you talking about? I saw nothing."

"You mean you didn't see it—you didn't hear it scream?"

"I don't know what you are talking about," she said. "Really, Mr. Anderson, this strikes me as a very silly attempt to frighten me."

"Frighten *you?*" he exclaimed. He hesitated a

minute longer, wiping his forehead, then went to the window, threw it up, and started to climb out.

"Wait!" said Mrs. Church. "You haven't got the reward for returning the necklace."

Mr. Anderson was outside by this time. "I'll stay right here," he said. "You can bring it to me."

So Mrs. Church got her purse and went back to the window. "It has to be one third of the value of the necklace," she said, "but I've decided to make it a little more."

"That's very good of you," he replied.

"Not at all," she said. "I'm sure you deserve something for your trouble." And she put a dime in his hand.

He stared at it. "I don't get it," he said. "What's this for?"

"I'm afraid, Mr. Anderson," she said with a smile, "that you—or rather, the burglar, didn't look very carefully at this necklace. I paid twenty-five cents for it. Really, I think ten cents is a rather generous third, don't you? If you know anything about fractions," she added maliciously.

"What!" he exclaimed. "I don't believe you! This is a very shabby trick, Mrs. Church. I brought back your necklace in good faith—"

"Indeed?" she said. "Well, give me back the

dime. And if you'd rather have the necklace, here it is. Now you and your burglar friend can sell it and live in luxury on the proceeds. Good day, Mr. Anderson." And she shut the window.

Freddy came back into the parlor to find Mrs. Church shaking with laughter. "It was lucky you said you didn't hear anything when I pulled that cloak down over my head," he said. "I wonder what he thinks now. Of course that was all a lie about his mysterious visitor this morning who brought the stolen necklace. I had a report from Jacob just before I got here, and nobody has visited his house except the delivery boy from Molecule's grocery. Anderson took that necklace himself. But I'd like to know how he got in."

"So would I," said Mrs. Church. "It's a funny thing: all these burglaries I've been reading about in the paper lately—they seem to have been done in the same way: nobody can figure out how the burglars got in. But I don't see how . . . unless Mr. Anderson is a member of a gang—"

"There couldn't be any connection," Freddy said. "I think Anderson just picked up your necklace in the course of doing his haunting. He just saw it and thought it was a good idea. And did you notice how red his eyes were? Do you think he'd been crying?"

"Maybe he got some pepper in them some-where," said Mrs. Church. "But Freddy, how could he get in?"

Freddy didn't even try to look wise and put on the Great Detective expression. He just shook his head.

CHAPTER
11

The crime wave was something that had both-
ered Freddy a good deal. From Buffalo to Al-
bany, from Watertown to New York, houses had
been entered and valuables taken, yet the police had made no arrests and apparently hadn't
a single clue. Freddy didn't see how Mr. An-

derson could be responsible for all these thefts. It looked more like the work of a well-organized gang. If that was so, could Mr. Anderson have had anything to do with stealing Mrs. Church's necklace?

Freddy read the accounts of the robberies in the New York papers and tried to figure out a theory about them. In his own newspaper, the *Bean Home News,* he wrote an editorial on that subject. "What are our police doing?" he asked. "Do we pay them to stand idly by when our citizens are daily victimized by gangs of bold and insolent criminals who laugh and giggle contemptuously at the minions of the law?" And so on. But of course he didn't have any more idea than the police did what to do about it, for in not a single case was there a clue to show how the burglars had got in.

In the meantime the baseball practice had gone on, and it was now, in the games at the Bean farm with the Centerboro High boys, that all the practice in the mud and snow began to pay off. The Martians and the Boomschmidt brothers and the animals worked together as a team. The Martians still swung at everything, and Freddy let them. They got fewer and fewer hits, because Jason Brewer, who usually pitched for the school, had found out that they would reach as quickly for a ball six inches beyond the end of their bat as for one right over the middle. But Freddy still refused to correct the tendency. "You boys go right on swinging," he said. "I don't care whether you get hits or not—even when we play Tushville. You play it my way and we'll win. I'm going to give you two signals: one, to swing at everything; two, not to swing at anything, not even the good ones. You leave the rest to Tushville."

Every day or so one or two of the Tushville players, who were now almost ready to start their own playing season, drove over with Mr. Kurtz to watch and jeer at the Martian team. They laughed particularly at Freddy, who was of course pretty funny looking, in the long black coat, with the big spectacles, and the white beard that came foaming out under the battered hat. He nearly always had Jinx or Mr. Pomeroy with him to act as his eyes as he stumbled about, leaning on his stick and peering at the players he was trying to coach. Fortunately Jinx knew a good deal more about baseball than Freddy did—although if Jinx had been coach, it is doubtful if he would ever have thought up Freddy's scheme for beating Tushville.

As the days got warmer, Freddy found his disguise more and more uncomfortable. At times he would turn the coaching over to Jinx and watch the practice as himself. One afternoon when practice was over he walked back to the flying saucer with Two-clicks. He hadn't entirely given up trying to question the Martians about the whereabouts of Squeak-squeak, although they refused to answer, and indeed avoided his company where before they had seemed to like to be with him. So today he said: "What do you hear from Squeak-squeak?"

"We hear—is well," said the Martian. Then, changing the subject: "You think we lick Tushers?"

"Sure," said Freddy confidently. "We lick." He had got in the habit of talking to the Martians in the same kind of broken English they used. Of course it wasn't helping them to learn to talk good English, but it was fun, and they understood it better than correct speech. "You do like Mr. Arquebus say, we lick."

Two-clicks shrugged all four of his shoulders. He was not convinced. But he didn't say any more. He climbed up on the disk of the saucer, which was made of some light shiny metal like stainless steel, opened the door in the turret, and with a wave to Freddy vanished inside.

As the pig turned to go, he glanced at the edge of the saucer near where it rested on the ground. Along that edge was a rusty-red stain. And all at once it came to Freddy—the stain was paint from Mrs. Church's tin roof, and it was out of the saucer, hovering close to the upper window, that the burglar had stepped when he stole the necklace.

So the Martians were the burglars! Freddy half turned to go back and confront Two-clicks with the proof of his guilt. Then he stopped. He had to think what he was going to do. So he went down to the cow barn to see Mrs. Wiggins.

"It looks pretty plain," he said. "Anderson could have got into the house without leaving any tracks if they'd brought him in the saucer. That darn thing can hover like a helicopter. One edge touched the roof and the red paint stuck to it."

"I guess Anderson was the ghost all right," said the cow, "but maybe it was the Martians that stole the necklace. They seem like nice little fellers, but good land, we don't know what kind of a bringing up they've had. Maybe they don't think it's wrong to steal."

"I can't really believe they would," Freddy said. "They might think it was funny to play ghost. . . . Golly," he said, "maybe Anderson *made* 'em do it. Maybe he threatened them somehow."

"Look, Freddy," said Mrs. Wiggins, "do you remember how Anderson got the rats to work

"Good day, Madam," a voice interrupted.

for him? He kidnapped one of them, and locked him up, and then threatened to do something awful to him if they wouldn't do as he said? Well, wasn't it you that was telling me that criminals always follow the same pattern —go to work in the same way? Why couldn't he have kidnapped Squeak-squeak?"

"I believe you've got it!" Freddy exclaimed. "My goodness, of course. And you remember the peanuts? He bought some the other day, and yet when I offered him some, he said he never used 'em. Who was he buying them for, then? If he's got Squeak-squeak—"

"Good day, madam," a voice interrupted. "Good day, pig. How is you both today?"

Freddy turned to see Leo in the doorway. "How *is* you!" he exclaimed. "What kind of baby-talk is that?"

"I . have . to . talk . like . that," said the lion. He spaced his words as if he was choosing them with great care, as if he didn't know the English language very well. "Mist—that is— the chief said last night I talked too much. I said how can I stop? I have to talk when I have things to say. He said: 'I know how. When you talk, leave out one let—one piece of the alphabet.' I said: 'O.K., I'll leave out *x*. Or *q*.' He said no, that wasn't fa—honest. He said I should leave out the eighteenth piece."

"Oh, I see," said Freddy. "You're leaving out *r*."

"Yes. But I said I wouldn't do it unless he did too. So he said he would leave out *t*. Boy, you should listen to him. Has he found some fancy words!"

"That sounds like fun," Mrs. Wiggins said. "Guess I'll try it. What letter shall I leave out?"

"Try *e*," said Freddy. "Now let's hear you say something."

"All right," said the cow. "This isn't so hard. Mr. Boomschmidt—"

"You can't say 'mister,'" Freddy interrupted.

"Good land, of course I can. It's just Capital *M*, *r*."

"It has an *e* in it," said the pig. "When you say it."

"Oh, all right," said Mrs. Wiggins slowly. "Captain Boomschmidt—" She stopped. "Oh, gracious! What was I going to say? It's gone— No, no; it's— Ha, I got it! it's vanished—vanisht with a *t*—out of my mind. Whew! I mean wow! That's too hard."

"Well, you took the hardest letter," said Freddy, who didn't remind her that he had picked it out. "*E* is used oftener in English than any other letter."

"Take *s*," Leo suggested.

"But then I can't talk about more than one of anything," said the cow. "Plurals are made with *s*."

"Shucks, there are lots of plurals without *s* —men, mice, oxen, women, deer—"

"But I don't want to talk about mice and men and oxen all the time. Suppose I want to talk about pigs. Do I say pice? Or what would be the plural of henhouse? Henhice?"

"Well," said Leo, "if you want to talk about two pigs, you can say 'a pig and a pig.'"

"I could say two piggen."

"The chief says that kind of thing is not allowed. I said: couldn't I talk like folks down South: couldn't I say: 'Mistah Boomschmidt is heah'? But he said that wasn't playing the game."

"You could talk baby-talk," said Freddy. "I saw thwee wats wunning awound on the wace-twack. Though I suppose it would sound kind of silly coming from a lion."

"No," said Leo, "he said that was out too. And I can't talk Chinaman talk either. You know: 'thlee lats lunning alound the lace tlack.' Well, it's kind of fun, at that. Why don't you tr—attempt it, pig?"

"I will, later. Right now we've got to check on this guy Anderson. We've had a tail on him, but that hasn't got us anywhere. We've got to get inside his house and search it. He may have Squeak-squeak locked up there. The A.B.I. has inspected the outside of the house and peeked in the windows, but to get inside we'll have to use our own people. Are the Webbs home, Mrs. W.?"

Mr. and Mrs. Webb were two elderly spiders who lived part of the year in the farmhouse, and the rest of the time in the cow barn. They had traveled extensively, had taken the famous trip to Florida with the other animals, and had visited Hollywood—had even appeared in the movies. But you would never have guessed it from their conversation, for they were modest, home-loving people, who would have been ashamed to appear to brag about their experiences. Mr. Webb had even written a book, *How to Make Friends and Influence Spiders,* which Mr. Brooks, the historian of the Bean farm, was using *his* influence to get published. Mr. Webb felt that too many people disliked spiders, and were inclined to swat them with a rolled-up newspaper rather than to engage them in friendly conversation. As a spider, he felt that they could, and should, be treated with consideration, that their reputation for bad temper was unjust, and that their friendship could be valuable. "Remember," he says in his introduction, "spiders are people. And people make good friends. Without people, you would have no friends; remember that." "Remember," he says again, "you have to *make* friends. Friends don't just come ready-made." Which is really a very deep saying.

"I think they are home," Mrs. Wiggins said. "Webb," she called, "come down here a minute. Freddy want— I mean would like to talk to you."

And presently, spinning down on a long strand from the roof, came the spider. He landed on Freddy's nose, crawled up to his ear, and said in his tiny voice: "Well, Freddy, what can I do for you?"

Mrs. Wiggins had told the Webbs about the ghost and the burglary at Mrs. Church's, so that Freddy made his explanation as short as possible. "And we'd like you to search Anderson's house. If you will, I'll take you down there tonight."

"Dear me," said Mr. Webb, "Mrs. Webb's Cousin Clifford and his wife are here on a visit for a few days. They live with Miss McMinnicle, down the road, you know. We can't very well run out on them. Mother's very fond of Cliff's wife, though"—he gave a tiny snicker— "we feel that her hostess gift was perhaps a trifle on the ostentatious side. An enormous

June bug—although really a couple of nice flies would have been enough."

"Maybe they'd like to go along," Freddy said. "Might make a nice change for them, and a touch of adventure. And of course, you'll be perfectly safe."

"H'm," said Mr. Webb, "that might be an idea. Our little web is rather close quarters for four grown spiders, not to speak of the eight children. Wait a minute." And he swarmed back up into the roof.

After a minute or two he was down again. "It's all right," he said. "They think it might be quite a little adventure for them. Mrs. Wiggins can look after the children. We'll spin a web over there under the window, and they can play there till we come back. What time do you want us to be ready?"

CHAPTER

12

It wasn't easy for the Webbs and their cousins to get into Mr. Anderson's house. The windows were screened, the door fitted tightly at the bottom, and there were no cracks in the foundation wall. There appeared to be a fire in the furnace still, so the chimney was no good.

To Mr. Webb, the tightness of the house
seemed suspicious. "Man's got something to
hide," he said, "when he takes such pains to
keep even a spider out. Confound the fellow!
What's he afraid of?"

"Now, Father, don't be impatient," said Mrs.
Webb. "All we've got to do is wait over the
front door and drop on his hat when he comes
home. In the meantime, we might have a nice
game of twenty questions." So Mr. Webb
started, and he chose the first fly that Cousin
Clifford had ever caught, and he was quite put
out when, just as they'd reached the nineteenth
question and hadn't guessed it, Mr. Anderson
came up the walk. But when he unlocked the
front door the spiders dropped on his hat and
were carried into the house.

It is quite a job to search a house. Mr. Webb
stayed with Mr. Anderson and rode around on
his coat collar, while the others started to search
the living room. Cousin Clifford and his wife
weren't much help. Cliff was of a literary turn,
and he got interested in the titles of the books
in the bookcase, and even tried to crawl between
the leaves of one or two to see what they were
about. And his wife ran to each of the windows
in turn, and then called out: "Oh, Clifford!
Come see this beautiful view! Isn't it pictur-
esque? Isn't it just like that lovely calendar in

Miss McMinnickle's kitchen? Oh, Clifford; I would like to live here. Couldn't we, Clifford?" Mrs. Webb left them arguing and went on into the kitchen.

But it was Clifford's wife who got them into trouble. Mr. Anderson went to the ice box and got out a bottle of root beer. He poured it into a glass and went into the living room and sat down. He drank half of it, and then he said: "Ha!" in a contented voice, and leaned back and closed his eyes.

Cousin Clifford's wife said: "Oh, Clifford, I have never tasted root beer. I think I shall try just a teeny little sip." And she dropped down off the window sill and ran across the floor and up Mr. Anderson to the glass around which his hand was still clasped. She got on the edge of the glass and leaned over to try to reach the root beer, which was nearly halfway down. And she fell in.

Well, there she was, standing on an ice cube —like Eliza crossing the ice in *Uncle Tom's Cabin*—and she couldn't possibly reach to the rim of the glass. She tried jumping, but the ice was too slippery and she just slid and fell into the root beer.

Cousin Clifford's wife was not very strong-minded. She pulled herself out of the root beer, and instead of trying again, she just sat down on the ice cube and burst into tears. Cousin Clifford didn't see her; he had climbed up the wall to admire Mr. Anderson's high school diploma, which hung over the fireplace. But Mr. Webb had seen, and he hurried down from Mr. Anderson's coat collar.

At first he thought perhaps he could hang onto the rim of the glass and let himself down inside so that she could catch hold of his hind legs. But she was too far down. He stood there thinking, on Mr. Anderson's cuff—and just then Mr. Anderson opened his eyes and his fingers tightened on the glass, and Mr. Webb knew that he was going to take another drink of root beer. If he did that, Cousin Clifford's wife would be swallowed, and that would be the end of her. With Mr. Webb, to think was to act. Without a moment's hesitation he walked down onto Mr. Anderson's wrist and bit him hard.

Spiders don't like to bite people—not so much because they are kind-hearted as because they don't like the taste. But if it was a question of saving a life, no real spider would hesitate. Mr. Webb did not specially like Cousin Clifford's wife; he thought she was pretty tiresome; but he supposed that Cousin Clifford would miss her if she was swallowed. So he bit. And, as he had foreseen, Mr. Anderson's arm gave a hard jerk and the glass flew out of his hand and landed on the carpet without breaking. And Cousin Clifford's wife scampered off and hid under the table, where Cousin Clifford, who had at last seen what was going on, found her and comforted her and helped dry her off.

Mr. Anderson swore and rubbed his wrist, and he looked around for Mr. Webb, but the spider was back on his coat collar again. So he got a dishcloth and mopped up the root beer. Just then the phone rang and he went into his office to answer it.

"Yes," he said. "This is Ed. . . . Yes. Is he getting along all right?" For several minutes, Mr. Webb couldn't hear what was said. Then: "Sure, Herb, I should think he could have all he wants. But maybe I ought to buy 'em. . . . I'll bring 'em to your office. . . . Oh, those—yes, I want to see you about them. . . . Eh? Yes, I suppose we'd better not be seen together. I'll come out tomorrow." And he said good-by and hung up.

"Not much in that," Mr. Webb said to himself. "Some business deal, I suppose. . . . Aha, this is more like it!" For Mr. Anderson had gone over to the big safe in the corner and begun to turn the dial.

Mr. Webb knew something about safes and their combinations, as he did about most things,

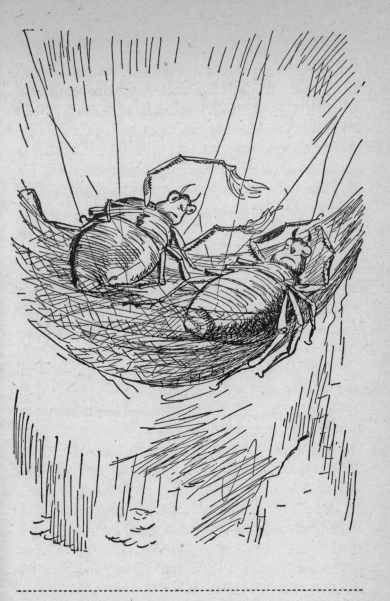

He spun her a sort of hammock.

and he noted carefully: three left, eighteen, four right, seven, two left, twenty-four. Then he gasped and nearly fell off Mr. Anderson's coat collar as the door swung open and he saw that the safe was nearly half full of a glittering mass of jewelry, flashing with rainbow hues of diamonds and emeralds and sapphires and rubies. He jumped to the floor and hurried off to find his wife.

Mrs. Webb, in the meantime, had searched the entire first floor and the cellar without finding any sign of Squeak-squeak, and she had gone up to the attic, leaving word with Cousin Clifford where she could be found. Cousin Clifford's wife was still very weak from her terrible experience on the ice cube, and her husband had helped her up the wall to a safe place behind Mr. Anderson's diploma. He spun her a sort of hammock so she could lie down, and then he stayed beside her and fanned her. "I'm so weak, Clifford," she kept saying. But she wasn't too weak to talk.

The door to the attic stairs was closed, but there was a crack above it wide enough for a spider to go through. Mr. Webb started across the ceiling toward it. Then he stopped. Down on the carpet where the root beer had been spilled he saw a fly. He spun down on a long strand of web and landed within a foot of the fly. "Hey," he said, "come here a minute, will you?"

The fly looked up. "Uh-uh," he said, and shook his head.

"Oh, don't be silly," said Mr. Webb. "I just want to ask you something. About Mr. Anderson."

"My mother told me never to talk to strangers," said the fly, and giggled.

"Very sensible advice," Mr. Webb agreed. "But all I want to know is—has Anderson had a prisoner here in the house, or has he said anything about a Martian named Squeak-squeak?"

"Did you say Squeak-squeak?" the fly asked. "What a silly name!" And he giggled some more.

"Look," said the spider, "be a little helpful, can't you?"

"Sure I can," the fly said, "but I'm not going to. Why should I? Help a spider? Ha! What did spiders ever do for me? Ate fourteen of my immediate family, that's what they did. And you've got the gall—"

"All right, all right," said Mr. Webb. Over the fly's shoulder he had seen Mrs. Webb creeping slowly toward him. She motioned to him to keep the fly occupied. "I suppose you're right," he went on. "There are, I believe, some spiders that eat flies—more shame to them, I say. I am, I am happy to assert, not numbered among them."

"Oh, yeah?" said the fly. "What do you eat?"

"Oh, this and that. Whatever happens to be handy. This root beer, now." He took a sip from a drop that had escaped Mr. Anderson's rag. "Delicious! Really, it makes me feel quite gay." He skipped a few dance steps, first to one side, then to the other, and behind the fly he could see Mrs. Webb put a forefoot up to her mouth to keep from laughing out loud as she crept closer. "But of course I don't suppose you know how to dance?" he said.

The fly knew perfectly well that he had no business even talking with a spider. But he was too vain and silly to let anyone suggest that he couldn't dance. "Pooh, that's nothing!" he said, and he duplicated Mr. Webb's steps.

"How about this one?" Mr. Webb leaped in the air and clapped all eight feet together.

Whether the fly would have attempted this Mr. Webb never found out, for Mrs. Webb was close now, and she jumped and caught him by the neck. "Tie him up, Father," she said, and while Mr. Webb spun several threads around him, she said: "Now, my smart young friend, perhaps you'll talk."

So of course he did. He told them that he had seen Squeak-squeak brought in the night he was kidnapped. Mr. Anderson had kept him for some time locked in the attic, but a day or two ago—the fly couldn't remember just what day it was—Anderson had taken him away somewhere in a car. "It can't be far," the fly said, "because he was only gone a couple of hours."

This, however, was the extent of the fly's information. Whether Mr. Anderson had gone out late at night in the saucer he didn't know, because he always went to sleep at dark. He didn't know anything about the safe and its contents either, because he never went into the office, where there were no crumbs.

When they had released the fly, Mrs. Webb told her husband that she had seen a lot of peanut shells in a room that was finished off in the attic, and it was apparent that someone had been staying there. "But we know now anyway that it was Squeak-squeak," she said. "But good gracious, Father, it's beginning to get dark. We'd better get ready to leave when Mr. Anderson goes out to his dinner. Freddy will be looking for us."

So they rounded up Cousin Clifford and his

wife, who was feeling better, but still weak, and stationed themselves over the front door, where they could drop on Mr. Anderson's hat when he went out.

And Mr. Anderson went out the back door.

CHAPTER
13

Freddy came back for the spiders at seven, the time when he knew that Mr. Anderson would be having supper at Dixon's Diner. But the spiders weren't on the gatepost, where they had agreed to wait. While he was standing there, wondering what to do, Rabbit No. 23 came out of the shrubbery and hopped up to him.

"The Webbs are still in there," he said. "They have been trying to attract my attention. Look, you can see 'em now." And he pointed at the office window. A black speck was swinging like a pendulum back and forth across the glass in the office window. When Freddy went closer, he could see that it was a spider hanging to a strand of web that was fastened to the top of the window.

"You can go up on the porch," said 23. "Anderson's a heavy feeder, he won't be back for a good three-quarters of an hour."

Close to the window, Freddy saw that it was Mrs. Webb swinging. Mr. Webb, on the side of the window, would push her when she swung back toward him. They seemed to be having fun, and he thought they were smiling at him—though it is pretty hard to tell with a spider unless you have a magnifying glass.

After a minute Mrs. Webb stopped, and both spiders ran to the corners of the window and scrabbled with their forefeet, as if trying to get out. Then they looked at Freddy and shook their heads.

"You mean you can't get out?" Freddy said in a loud voice.

They could hear him, but of course they knew he couldn't hear anything they said with the window between them. So they nodded.

Then Mrs. Webb pointed at Mr. Webb, who hopped to the floor and started toward the safe. She kept pointing at him as he climbed up onto the dial and went around it in first one direction then the other.

"You mean you know the combination?" Freddy asked, and she nodded.

"What good does that do?" he asked.

Well, the Webbs tried every way they could to tell Freddy about the jewelry. They hung imaginary necklaces around their necks, and imaginary bracelets on their legs; they held imaginary jewelry out and shaded their eyes to show how blindingly it glittered—but Freddy just shook his head hopelessly. Then they tried to show him by gestures that he must break the window and come in. Freddy understood that, but when he had asked them if Squeak-squeak was there, and they had shaken their heads, he said no, he wasn't going to break in. "You stay by the back door, after Anderson gets back," he said. "I'll get you out."

He knew that Jinx was at Mrs. Peppercorn's and he hurried over there. The cat often came into town in the evening to go to the movies, and he usually stopped in for a chat with the old lady beforehand. They had been friends ever since they had taken the famous trip around the solar system together in the Benjamin Bean Space Ship. Jinx never tired of listening to Mrs. Peppercorn's terrible poetry, although Freddy's verses, which really rhymed, just put him to sleep.

When he reached the house, Jinx and Mrs. Peppercorn were coming down the steps. "Ah, good evening, Frederick—good evening," said the cat. He always put on a good deal of manner when he was escorting a lady. "Lovely evening, is it not?"

"Hello, Mrs. P.," said Freddy. "Look, Jinx, I've got a job for you. Will you—"

"Tut, tut, my dear fellow," said the cat. "Don't you see that I am occupied? Mrs. Peppercorn has consented to accompany me to the cinema. Another time, dear chap; another time." And to Mrs. Peppercorn: "Madam, if you please," and he stood aside for her to pass out through the gate, then paced along beside her, his tail waving genteelly.

Mrs. Peppercorn tried to match Jinx's dignity, but she was unable to suppress a faint cackle of laughter, which she tried to smother behind her hand.

But Freddy didn't give up. "I'm sorry to intrude," he said, "but this is really very important, Jinx. The Webbs are in trouble. I'm sure Mrs. Peppercorn will excuse you. You can join her at the—the cinema in half an hour."

"My dear old pig," said the cat, "you don't understand. I see that you are unaccustomed to polite language. If I *must* descend to your own vulgar level, why I must. You will forgive me, madam," he said to Mrs. Peppercorn. Then to Freddy: "Beat it, you dope!" he yelled. "Scram!"

There wasn't much to be done with Jinx when he was in this mood, but fortunately Mrs. Peppercorn came to Freddy's rescue. "Oh, come along, Jinx! Do as Freddy asks you to. The Webbs are friends of yours, aren't they? I'll go to the movie and you come later."

Jinx stood up on his hind legs to make her a courtly bow, with a paw over his heart. "Your wish is my law, madam," he said. "But I insist on escorting you as far as the cinema."

So Jinx and Freddy walked with her to the movie theater, then went on to Mr. Anderson's.

"What's with old Webb?" the cat asked. "I've always told him he ought to lay off this chasing flies. Some of these flies around here are tough customers. What happened—one bite him in the leg?"

Freddy explained, and then told Jinx what he wanted him to do. As he had expected, the cat was delighted. "Golly, I'm glad you came for me. The movie wasn't anything special—just one of those corny super-enormous-colossal riots with Cleopatra and Henry the Eighth and a lot of elephants. . . . There's Anderson, sitting at his desk. Do you suppose it's dark enough to go to work on him?''

Freddy thought it was, and they sneaked down past the side of the house into the back yard. Freddy hid in some shrubbery at the side of the back porch, and Jinx climbed up on the back fence. ''Too bad there ain't a moon,'' he said. ''I always put more feeling into it in the moonlight.'' Then he threw back his head and began to yowl.

''Golly,'' Freddy said to himself, ''if he put any more feeling into it, they'd call out the National Guard.'' And indeed those who heard it said afterward that they were shaken to the depths of their souls. It brought heads to back windows all down the block; it brought Mr. Anderson dashing out of his back door, so that the spiders walked out without being noticed; unfortunately for Jinx, it brought Dr. Wintersip, who lived directly back of Mr. Anderson, dashing out of *his* back door. And both Dr. Wintersip and Mr. Anderson had snatched up the first thing that was the right size for throwing, and they both threw. Jinx, caught between two fires, was unable to dodge. Mr. Anderson's frying pan missed him by an eighth of an inch, sailed over the fence and grazed Dr.

Jinx, caught between two fires, was unable to dodge.

Wintersip's left ear. But Dr. Wintersip's bottle of ketchup whizzed past the cat's nose and hit Mr. Anderson square on the chin, knocking him flat and drenching him with ketchup.

Dr. Wintersip heard Mr. Anderson yelp. He came to the fence and looked over, and in the light that streamed from the back door, saw Mr. Anderson lying there, covered with ketchup. He didn't realize that the cap had been off the ketchup bottle when he picked it up. "Blood!" he said. "Oh, my goodness! Oh, my gracious!" and he scrambled over the fence.

Mr. Anderson sat up as Dr. Wintersip bent over him. "Wha-what are you doing in my bedroom?" he demanded shakily. Then he put his hand to his face and brought it away dripping with ketchup. He stared at it a moment, then fell back with a groan and apparently passed out again.

"Oh dear!" said Dr. Wintersip. "Oh dear, oh dear, oh dear!"

In the meantime, Freddy and Jinx had sneaked around and up on the porch, where the spiders were waiting. Freddy had a bad sneezing fit when all four of them dropped onto his nose, but Dr. Wintersip was still wringing his hands over the apparently unconscious Mr. Anderson and didn't even look up.

Mr. Webb quickly told Freddy about the

jewelry in the safe. "If you want to get it, I've got the combination."

"The back door's open," said Jinx. "What are we waiting for?"

If Freddy had thought about it a minute, he probably wouldn't have gone in. But here was a chance, and probably the only chance, to solve at one stroke the mysterious burglaries that had baffled the police of nearly every big city in the state. By the time Mr. Anderson, groaning and leaning heavily on Dr. Wintersip's shoulder, had been helped into his living room and made comfortable on a couch, Freddy had the safe open and was piling the jewelry into a waste-basket that stood beside the desk.

Dr. Wintersip went out into the kitchen and got towels and a pan of warm water. But when he started to clean up Mr. Anderson, he stopped suddenly. In the lighted room it was plain that the red liquid which hid Mr. Anderson's features was not out of Mr. Anderson's veins but out of a ketchup bottle. He hesitated. "Dear me," he said to himself. "Mr. Anderson is going to be angry when he finds out that I hit him with a bottle. Also, he is going to feel very silly when he realizes that he fainted away because he had ketchup all over his face. An angry man who has made a fool of himself is not really very good company. I think I will leave." And he quietly put the pan of water down on the floor, dropped the towels beside it, and tiptoed out.

And Freddy and Jinx tiptoed out after him. Nobody saw them. Nobody passed them on the street as they carried the wastebasket down to Mrs. Peppercorn's, and nobody, Freddy said, could possibly know that the jewelry was now in the bottom drawer of the dresser in Mr. Arquebus's room.

"Why don't you sign up old Wintersip to pitch for your Martians," Jinx said. "He sure throws a mean ketchup bottle."

"I wish we'd found Squeak-squeak instead of the jewelry," said Freddy. "Of course it's nice to have pinned all those burglaries on Anderson. And there are big rewards offered for some of the stuff, too. But we still don't know where Squeak-squeak is."

"Anderson will probably have an alibi for every one of those burglaries," said Jinx. "With that saucer to travel in, he could get to Buffalo and pull a job and be back home in half an hour. Nobody'd believe that he'd have had time to do it."

"Maybe not. But how's he going to explain having the stuff in his safe? We could take it right to the sheriff tonight. But I think we ought to get Squeak-squeak back first."

"I guess you're right," said the cat. "Well, Webb has told us about the phone conversation he overheard. Somebody named Herb, and they ought not to be seen together. Well, how do you like Herb Garble for the guy that has Squeak-squeak?"

"I like him fine," Freddy said. "I like him so much that—" He stopped. "Hey, Webb," he said. "How'd you like to search another house tonight? Where Mr. Garble lives?"

Mr. Garble lived with his sister, Mrs. Underdunk. They were probably the only enemies Freddy had in all Centerboro—which on the whole viewed its talented neighbor with pride and affection. Freddy had had a great deal of trouble with them. They had been in several plots to injure him, and even to ruin the Beans. And though he had defeated these, it had been at considerable danger to himself. Mr. Garble seemed the likeliest accomplice for Mr. Anderson.

But at Mrs. Underdunk's they drew a blank. Getting in was easy—there was a wide crack under the front door. Mr. and Mrs. Webb and Cousin Clifford went in, leaving Cousin Clifford's wife in care of Freddy—Mr. Webb said she was more bother than she was worth. They spent two hours searching the house from top to bottom, even the jam closet in the cellar where Freddy had once been imprisoned—but there was no sign of Squeak-squeak—not so much as one peanut shell.

"It's begun to rain, and I guess we'd better call it a day," Freddy said, when the spiders came out. "We'll go back to Mrs. Peppercorn's, and then tomorrow I'll take you Webbs back home."

But an unpleasant surprise awaited them at Mrs. Peppercorn's. Freddy's room was in disorder. The mattress was dragged off the bed, bureau drawers were pulled out and their contents scattered about the floor—and the jewelry was gone.

"Hey, look here," said Jinx. There was mud on the window sill, and under the window the print of a shoe sole—one that Freddy remembered, with a herringbone pattern on the sole and a triangle on the heel.

"Anderson!" Freddy said. "Now how could he know that we had the jewelry? Or rather, that Mr. Arquebus had it? He couldn't possibly have known that it would be here."

"You don't suppose that he could have seen us going out with that jewelry?" said Jinx.

"He was in a dead faint when we left with the stuff," said Freddy. "And even if he had seen us, he doesn't know that I'm Mr. Arquebus. I just don't see *how*—" Freddy stopped short. "Oh, gosh!" he said suddenly. "I've got it! I know what happened. He wasn't after the jewelry at all—probably didn't know it wasn't still in his safe. No, what he came here for was the wallet full of money he thought I had."

CHAPTER

14

Whatever Mr. Anderson may have thought about his safe being opened, and the jewelry taken by Mr. Arquebus, he didn't say anything to that gentleman. He kept right on coming up to the farm nearly every day to watch the baseball practice. Mr. Pomeroy was much disturbed at the failure of his A.B.I. operatives to find out how Mr. Anderson had managed to leave, and return to, his house without being observed, but as Freddy pointed out, it was so unusual for anyone to have a flying saucer pick him up at an upper window that they might well be excused for not having spotted it. Several sharp-eyed night-flying moths had now been posted at all the upstairs windows, but Mr. Anderson's nocturnal excursions had evidently been discontinued.

Freddy, however, decided to have it out with Two-clicks, so he called him one afternoon into the cow barn for a conference with Mrs. Wiggins, Jinx, Leo, and J. J. Pomeroy. Freddy didn't beat about the bush. He told the Martian that he knew that the saucer had been taking Mr. Anderson on midnight trips all over the state, to burglarize the houses of rich people and steal their valuables. He told him all he had found out. "And how do you think Mr. Boomschmidt will like that?" he said.

Two-clicks rolled his third eye and waved his feelers agitatedly. "You not tell Mr. Boom," he said. "We no can help. Mr. Andyson he grab Squeak-squeak, he say, we no do like he want, we no see Squeak-squeak again. He make us go burgling. We no like. But we don't can stop it, is it?"

"No, I guess it isn't," Freddy said.

The discussion that followed was somewhat hampered by the fact that Mrs. Wiggins could not use the letter *s*, Leo, the letter *r*, and Mr. Pomeroy, who had also got interested in the game, the letter *g*. They had all really become quite expert at it, but since they were thinking less about what they were saying than about how they were going to say it without using their letter, they didn't always make sense.

"If you could only find out where our kidnapped friend wa—I mean, became locked up," said Mrs. Wiggins, "we would have a chance to resc—I mean, relea—I mean, get him out."

"Anderson talked on the phone to somebody named Herb, and it sounded as if he was talking about Squeak-squeak," said Freddy. "The only Herb I can think of is Mr. Garble, but the Webbs searched his house and didn't find anything."

"Our operatives," said Mr. Pomeroy, "have been unable to find any connection between Anderson and Mr.—ah, Mrs. Underdunk's brother. We have watched this man carefully, and all his time for the past few days has been accounted for. I will stake my reputation," said Mr. Pomeroy forcefully, "that he does not know anyth—that he is not concerned in this crime."

"You maybe find it somebody else got name

Herb?" inquired Two-clicks.

"I can think of four or five in Centerboro," Freddy said. "But I don't think any of them could have had anything to do with Anderson. Still, we ought to investigate them. Eh, J.J.?"

"Hand me their names," said Mr. Pomeroy, "and I'll attend to it."

"Please, you not tell somebody I tell about Mr. Andyson," Two-clicks begged. "He say, we tell, Squeak-squeak not come ever back. Not ever, ever, ever."

"Don't you worry," said Mrs. Wiggins. "We don't—won't—" She stopped. She couldn't think of a phrase that didn't have an *s* in it. She thought of: we won't say a word; we won't discuss it; we won't speak of it. . . . All esses. . . .

"We won't tell anybody about it," Freddy suggested.

"Drat it!" said the cow. "Why couldn't I think of that?"

"You don't tell nobody neither, is it, Leo?" the Martian inquired.

"If I don't tell nobody, that means I do tell somebody, doesn't it?" said the lion.

"Huh?" said Two-clicks.

"Skip it, kid," said Leo. "My Uncle Ajax always said: Never explain a weak joke. Just change the subject quick."

"You used an *r*," said J. J.

"I was quoting my uncle," Leo replied.

"We won't give you away, Two-clicks," said Freddy. "But if you find out anything at all from Anderson, do please tell us. If you'd trusted us in the first place, you'd have been better off."

"You right, I guess it," Two-clicks admitted.

The conference bumbled along, getting nowhere, a while longer. They broke up finally without deciding anything more than that they ought to look for somebody named Herb. "'The Case of the Missing Martian' becomes 'The Case of the Guilty Herb,' " Freddy said to Mr. Pomeroy.

"Have no doubts," said the robin. "We shall find him."

"I hope you're right," said Freddy.

Two-clicks patted the pig consolingly on the back with a couple of his hands. "I t'ink so you find Squeak-squeak. I sorry don' tol' you right away. Mr. Andyson, he scare we. He very mad—oh, he holler very loud! Yes, yes! He scare Squeak-squeak. Squeak-squeak write letter—say we not telling you, not telling nobody."

Freddy said he guessed under the same circumstances he would not have disclosed the identity of Squeak-squeak's captor either.

"Huh?" said Two-clicks.

"I guess I do same like you done," Freddy said. "I not tell nobody nothing neither."

"Sure," said the Martian.

During the next few days Freddy was too busy with preparations for the first game with Tushville to hunt for clues to the whereabouts of Squeak-squeak. The A.B.I., of course, were continuing their efforts, and Mr. Pomeroy, combing through the Centerboro phone book, had turned up four more Herberts, whom he was having investigated. Mr. Boomschmidt had agreed with Mr. Kurtz that the winning team should take two thirds of the gate receipts, and he and Freddy—disguised of course as Mr. Arquebus—had driven over in the saucer to inspect the Tushville diamond, where the game was to be played.

On the day of the game, Freddy got himself up very carefully. All Tushville was expected to turn out, and certainly all Centerboro would drive over to root for the Martians. And there would be people from all over—Aeschylus Center and Gomorrah Falls and South Pharisee and Plutarch Mills, and probably even Rome and Syracuse and Utica. So Freddy had Mademoiselle Rose press his coat, and then she washed his beard and ironed it. Leo, who had been to the beauty shop and had his mane washed and set, wanted Freddy to go with him and have a wave put in his beard, but the pig said no. "'Tisn't dignified," he said. "Not for old Henry Arquebus, it ain't. And for goodness' sake," he added, "don't let 'em drench you with cheap perfumery this time. You go round smelling like a wilted bouquet. If you aren't careful, somebody'll throw you in the trash can."

Although the Boomschmidt Martians didn't have any uniforms, they certainly made a nice appearance when they marched onto the field. Freddy had bought some white doll boots, and Henrietta led the procession in them, as a drum majorette. Next came the five Martians, then Oscar and Leo, with Mr. Hercules between them, juggling the iron cannonballs as he walked. And finally old Hannibal, with a little house on his back containing Mr. Boomschmidt and Mr. Arquebus.

As soon as they had broken ranks and started warming up, Henrietta ran across to the section of the bleachers where the animals from the Bean farm were seated. She picked up a megaphone and led them in a cheer. This was a sneezing routine which Freddy had suggested to her, basing it upon Mr. Anderson's performance when the pepper went up his nose. It went rather like this: "A—a—a—chew! A—a—a—chee!

Henrietta led the procession.

A—a—a—chaw!. . . Hup . . . hup . . . hup
. . . CHOW!" Henrietta led it with a remark-
ably fine display of acrobatic skill, and on the
final "CHOW!" turned a complete somersault.
Charles was so amazed that he hardly paid any
attention to the game, but kept saying to his
companions: "Where on earth did she learn
that?" and "Good gracious, can that be my
Henrietta?" all the rest of the afternoon.

The Tushville team, although in brand-new
uniforms and accompanied by the Tushville
band, did not get the applause that the Martians
did. But that was because there were so many
strangers, hundreds, who had seen uniformed
teams often enough, but never before a team
composed of circus animals and creatures from
another planet.

Tushville won the toss. The first batter up
was a man with a black beard who, although he
was married and had three children, had played
on the Tushville High School football team two
years earlier. Freddy remembered him well; he
was a dirty player, and he had slugged Freddy
every time he had got a chance until at last the
pig got angry and bit him in the leg. Then
Black Beard had quit the game.

Chirp-squeak's first pitch was straight over
the plate. But Black Beard, although he had
been over to watch some of the practice at the

Bean farm, was confused by the Martian's four arms. And when an arm on the other side delivered the second pitch, he still didn't swing, although it was slow and he couldn't have missed. With two strikes on him, he got mad. He swung too hard at the third pitch, missed it by inches, and was out.

The second man up was Smith, the Tushville pitcher, who was suspected of being Zingwall, a professional pitcher in one of the minor leagues, hired by Tushville under an assumed name. He, too, was plainly puzzled by the four-arm delivery, but he didn't get confused. He waited out two balls and two strikes, and then hit a line drive over Oscar, the shortstop's, head, which put him safe on second. After which Ernie Popp, the catcher, singled, and Jaybob, the center fielder, struck out.

Cranbury, the shortstop, was the next man up. When he swung at the first one, Smith (or Zingwall) tried to steal third, but Mr. Boomschmidt caught Leo's throw and tagged him.

The Tushvillers groaned, for with two men on bases, even with two out, there had been a good chance to score. But Henrietta dashed out in front of the cheering section and led a cheer for Chirp-squeak. This included the Martian word for "Hurrah," which sounded sort of like "Wheeeeeech-click!" It is, of course, the Martians being such a gentle people, a very mild exclamation, much more like "Goody, goody," than "Hurrah." After this they sang one verse of the circus marching song, in honor of Mr. Boomschmidt.

Freddy's batting order did not at once reveal his secret method for winning the game. Hannibal led off. He didn't use a bat. He let two balls go by, then swung with his trunk at the third and sent it rolling down to the shortstop, who fielded it neatly and sent it straight to Black Beard, covering first. If Black Beard had stood his ground, Hannibal would have been out. But when he saw the elephant bearing down on him at a dead run, the man lost his nerve and stepped aside. He caught the throw, but he was nowhere near the sack when he did.

Mr. Boomschmidt followed, but the Tushville pitcher was too much for him—he fouled into the stand, and then misjudged two fast ones and twice hit nothing but air. Chirpsqueak, the poorest batter among the Martians, came up next. Freddy gave him the signal not to strike at anything, but when the Tushville catcher fumbled the first pitch, Hannibal tried to steal second and was put out. With two out, Freddy decided not to try for runs in that inning, and he gave the batter the "strike at everything" signal. The Martian quickly fanned himself back to the bench.

The first half of the second was much like the first: Oigle, Tushville right fielder, and Brown, second baseman, confused by trying to guess which of Chirp-squeak's four whirling hands would throw the ball, struck out. Agglett, the third baseman, just as confused as the others but more determined, swung wildly at each pitch, with the result that on the third one he connected and drove the ball over the left field fence for a home run. But then Black Beard came up again, and exactly repeated his former performance—he watched two go by, swung angrily at the third and missed by a mile.

With the score at Tushville 1, Martians 0, Freddy decided to let things go on a while before trying his trick scheme. So he signaled the three Martians who were next in batting order to continue swinging at everything. Smith realized that this was what they were doing, although he didn't know the reason, and he threw high and low and outside without caring much where the ball went as long as it didn't cross the plate. With the result that he struck out Chirp, Click-two-squeaks and Two-clicks, in that order. And in the first half of the third Tushville scored two runs.

But Freddy still held back his scheme. With Mr. Hercules, Leo, Hannibal, and Oscar coming up to bat, in that order, he couldn't at the moment do anything else, for the scheme depended for its success on having at least two Martians up in succession. Mr. Hercules grounded out, Leo fouled twice and then watched the third strike go past him, and Hannibal singled. When Oscar swung at the first pitch, Hannibal stole second, and when the ostrich swung again, he stole third. The third baseman had the ball in his hand before Hannibal got there, but the elephant slid. And when an elephant slides, something has to go. In this case it was the third baseman, who went six feet in the air, dropping the ball on the way up, and yelling for help on the way down. But Oscar struck out.

With Tushville having collected two more runs in the first half of the fourth, Mr. Boomschmidt came to bat for the Martians. Smith, feeling that the game was in the bag, had grown a little careless. He gave Mr. Boomschmidt his base on balls. That was more than Freddy had hoped for. "Now's our chance," he said to himself, and as Chirp-squeak stepped up to the plate, he gave him the signal which meant: "Don't strike at anything."

CHAPTER
15

Freddy's scheme was a simple one. A pitched ball, in order to be counted as a strike, has to go over the plate at a height below the batter's armpit, and above his knee. With even a small boy this distance isn't much less than two feet; with a grown man it is three feet or more. But a Martian is only two feet tall, and from his knee to his lower pair of armpits is not much more than eight inches. As long as the Martians continued to swing at everything, nobody paid much attention to this, but as soon as they stopped hitting at anything, Freddy figured that it would be pretty hard for even a good pitcher to put half his pitches across the plate and in that small strike zone. For of course to throw three strikes before he threw four balls, he would have to make half his throws good ones.

Smith's first pitch was a foot above Chirp-squeak's head. But the Martian didn't swing. "Ball!" shouted Mr. Bean, and threw up his left hand.

Smith hesitated a moment. Every ball he had thrown to one of the Martians before had been swung at—even one that had slipped from his hand as he threw and went halfway toward first base. Well, he thought, maybe the guy wasn't ready. He tried another high one.

"Ball two!"

At this, the catcher pulled off his mask and ran up, and he and Smith whispered together for a minute. They went back, and the next pitch was closer in.

"Ball three!" Chirp-squeak hadn't moved.

By this time, Smith realized that the Martian had decided to wait for a good one. But he had grown careless, pitching them anyhow, and he found it impossible to throw a strike into such a narrow target. He realized, too, that even if he were pitching at the top of his form, it would be beyond his skill to put these creatures out if they wouldn't reach for those that were a little out of range.

So Chirp-squeak got his base on balls, and Mr. Boom moved up to second. Then Chirp walked, and after him, Click-two-squeaks. And Mr. Boomschmidt walked home.

By this time Smith's pitching had improved somewhat, and he had begun to find the range. He had two strikes on Two-clicks before the Martian walked. And then Mr. Hercules came up.

Now Smith had a target that was probably five times as high, and he had no trouble in finding it. He put one right through the center, and Mr. Hercules' bat met it there and sent it sailing over center field for a home run. And that brought in three more Martians, making the score Tushville 5, Martians 6.

The excitement in the stands was intense. Henrietta led cheer after cheer, and turned so many somersaults that she became quite dizzy and had to be led back to a seat. Hannibal was the next batter up. He singled, and then Oscar came up and drove one right into the shortstop's hands for a double play. But Mars was still in the lead.

Smith slammed down his glove and came in, followed by the rest of the team, who crowded about Mr. Kurtz. The pitcher was furious.

"You get those midgets out of there," he shouted, "or I quit! I can't pitch to midgets."

"Oh, come," said Mr. Kurtz. "You've been over to watch 'em practice. You knew what size they were."

"Sure I did," the pitcher retorted, "but I didn't know they'd just stand there waiting for me to walk 'em."

"They're not obliged to try to get hits off you," said the manager.

"Look," said Smith, "you know what you're askin' me to do? You're askin' me to stand sixty feet from a target the size of the hole in a stovepipe and put a ball through it three times out of six. Because if they won't strike at anything, that's what I have to do. And there ain't any pitcher can do it."

"Oh, yeah?" said Mr. Kurtz sarcastically, "I notice you talked big enough about what you could do when I hired you. Well, you signed up with me, and win or lose, you're going to pitch these two games—understand?"

He would have said more, but Mr. Bean pushed his way through the knot of players, followed by Mr. Arquebus. "What we got here," he demanded, "a ball game or a debatin' society? Get your boys up there, Kurtz. Take a look up in the stands. Those folks'll be down here on the field in a minute, and if they do come down—"

"Get them so-called ball players of yourn up to the plate, Kurtz, dad rat ye," Freddy shouted. "Ye can't play baseball with your mouth."

"Oh, is that so?" Kurtz replied. "You played a trick on us, Arquebus. Ain't any pitcher can pitch strikes to a bunch of little spiders."

"Mebbe that's so and mebbe it ain't," said Freddy. "You thought you was playin' a trick on us, didn't you, concealin' the fact that three at least of your team are well-known players, playin' under assumed names? What's more, you knew these Martian boys were small, but you figured that it didn't matter, as long as they swung at everything."

"But they don't *ever* swing! They don't *try* to hit!" Kurtz protested almost tearfully.

"Ain't any law says they have to, is there?" Freddy demanded.

The stands were getting impatient. "Come on, Tushville; play ball!" they yelled. Even the Tushville rooters joined in the angry protests.

Mr. Anderson had appeared from somewhere. He took Mr. Kurtz's arm. "Look,

"What we got here, a ball game or a debatin' society?"

Kurtz," he said, "be a sport. You don't want to lose the game by default, do you? He bent and muttered something in the manager's ear. Freddy edged closer, trying to hear, but Anderson, bringing his arm up sharply as if to scratch his head, caught the pig a sharp blow under the chin with his elbow.

"Consarn ye, ye clumsy gowk!" Freddy exclaimed. He didn't forget, even with the surprise and pain of the blow, that he was Mr. Arquebus.

Anderson whirled on him. He appeared suddenly to have lost his temper completely. "You dirty thief!" he said under his breath, and pulled back his arm to punch the whiskered face.

Freddy got set to duck, but stood his ground. "Go ahead," he said. "Want me to tell everybody about what I got out of your safe?"

"Shut up, you fool!" Anderson whispered. And dropped his arm.

"I can talk or I can shut up," said Freddy. "It's all accordin'. Maybe you'd like to talk to me, instead of me talkin' to the cops. Maybe—"

Freddy had been aware for a minute or two of some large person pushing toward him through the crowd of excited players. Now he felt a huge hand resting lightly on his shoulder, and the heavy voice of Mr. Hercules said:

"Muster Arquebus, thus guntlemun a botherin' yuh?"

"Well, he's a spectator, Herc," Freddy said. "He ain't any business down here on the field. Maybe you'd escort him back to his seat."

So Mr. Hercules took hold of Mr. Anderson's collar with one hand and the slack of his pants with the other, and carried him, squirming and kicking, back into the grandstand and plunked him down in his seat.

When Freddy turned his attention again to Mr. Kurtz and his team, he found that they were dispersing. Smith had gone grumbling back to the bench, and Swiggett had stepped up to the plate and was waiting for the pitch.

In the fifth inning, Swiggett fouled out, Ernie Popp hit one over the fence for a home run, Jaybob singled, then he and Cranbury were put out on a double play. This evened the score. But the Martians came up in the same order as they had in the fourth. Mr. Boomschmidt struck out, but the four Martians again refused to try for anything that Smith could throw them, and again offered such small targets that he could not strike them out. One after the other they took their base on balls. Chirp-squeak was forced in, and the bases were loaded with Martians. By that time Smith was so nervous that he couldn't throw a strike even to Mr. Hercules, who was the next one up. The strong man hit a two bagger, Leo popped out, and Hannibal bunted and was put out, but not until the last of the Martians and Mr. Hercules had crossed the plate. And the score stood at Tushville 6, Martians 11.

The sixth was even worse for Tushville. Oigle singled, Brown struck out, and Agglett hit a fly to center field which Chirp caught easily. With two out, Black Beard evidently felt that he didn't have much chance. He swung half-heartedly at the first two pitches, waited out two wide ones, then hit a grounder straight into Oscar's huge claw. The ostrich swung back his foot so slowly that Freddy thought the man would reach first before the ball did. But Oscar was slow because he was taking careful aim. The claw swept forward and the ball went straight and true into Two-clicks' glove, so fast that it nearly knocked the Martian over. And a full second before Black Beard's toe touched first.

It was when the Martian team was coming in to bat that Mr. Hercules came over to where Freddy was sitting on the bench. "Mr. Arquebus," he said. " 'Tain't none of my business, but that there Underson, he's down here again. Want I should put um back in hus seat?"

Freddy looked across to where Two-clicks

had been stopped by Mr. Anderson as he was coming in from first. As he watched, they exchanged a few words, then the Martian nodded as if agreeing, and Anderson went back to the stand.

"He seems to have gone back, Herc," Freddy said. "But you might keep an eye on him."

He had forgotten to talk the way Mr. Arquebus was supposed to talk, and Mr. Hercules gave him a puzzled look. "Yuh remind me o' somebody, Mr. Arquebus," he said. "'S funny. Mus' be somebody Uh know, mustn't it? Don' seem's'ough Uh could be reminded of somebody Uh ain't uhquainted with, could Uh? Mebbe Uh could though, huh? Lumme see— who don't Uh know?"

Freddy left the strong man to the rather hopeless task of going over in his mind all the people he didn't know, and turned back to the game. Oscar had singled and was running for second. Mr. Boomschmidt was running toward first, but before he reached it, the ball, which he had driven straight into the second baseman's glove, was fielded to Black Beard. Then Chirp-squeak came to bat, and to Freddy's amazement, he swung at the first ball and missed.

Freddy at once began scratching his left ear, which was the signal for the Martians not to swing at anything. But Chirp-squeak paid no attention. He swung twice more, and was out.

Then Chirp came up. Freddy clawed frantically at his ear, but it was no good: Chirp also struck out.

Freddy stumbled out, holding his glasses up from his nose so that he could see under them, and stopped Two-clicks as he started out toward first. He demanded to know what they meant by disregarding his signals.

He understood Two-clicks to say that the Martians wanted to play the game like regular players, not just stand up at the plate and watch the pitches whiz by.

"But you are playing," he protested. "The point of the game is to get runs, not to swing at something you can't hit. And you've been getting runs; you've seen how it works."

But Two-clicks was not convinced. And they were holding the game up. Freddy had to let him go.

The rest of the game was a disaster. Mr. Boomschmidt and Freddy argued and argued with the Martians. But it did no good. Tushville got two runs in the seventh, but Click-two-squeaks and Two-clicks struck out, and Mr. Hercules, who followed them, was out when Jaybob caught a fly that he knocked into center field. In the eighth, Tushville got four runs—

owing mainly to the fact that Two-clicks and Click-two-squeaks fumbled every ball that was thrown to them. They not only fumbled them; they fell on them and couldn't find them, and when they found them, they made ridiculously wild throws. And Chirp-squeaks' pitching became just tossing the ball over the plate, so that the Tushville players almost knocked him out of the box. At the beginning of the ninth, with the score at 12—11 in favor of Tushville, Freddy took Chirp-squeak out and sent Mr. Hercules in to pitch. He sent a young alligator named Roger to take the strong man's place at right field. Roger was no good in the outfield, but he had shown some skill at batting, which he did with his tail.

But all this was too late to save the game. Tushville won, 13—11.

CHAPTER
16

Freddy was so discouraged at the defeat of the
Martian team that when he got back to Centerboro, instead of going out to the farm, he
sneaked away from his friends and went up
into the room he had rented at Mrs. Peppercorn's and sat down in a rocking chair by the

window. He didn't even take off his hat or his whiskers. He just sat there.

He had tried hard to be a good coach. He hadn't known much about baseball when he started, but he had read all the books he could find in the Centerboro Library on the subject, and had talked to the Centerboro High coach. And he did know a lot about team spirit—which is the thing that makes a group of nine players a team, not just a crowd. He felt that he had done a good job, too. The team had played well together. Until the Martians had quit.

There was a rap on the door and Mrs. Peppercorn put her head in. "What are you doing, sitting here all by yourself in the dark with your hat on?" she demanded.

Freddy said: "It isn't dark."

"Well, you look as if it ought to be," she said. "My land, don't you know that poem by Longfellow:

> *The day is done, and the darkness*
> *Falls from the wings of Night*
> *As a brick comes hurtling downward*
> *From a rooftop, in a fight."*

"That doesn't sound quite right," Freddy said.

"I changed it," said Mrs. Peppercorn. "I'm rewriting Longfellow's poems. He was a good poet all right, but he's kind of old-fashioned. I want to put some snap into him. In this one I change the meaning, but keep the same sound of the words. I haven't finished yet, but I've fixed up a couple of stanzas. Sort of repaired 'em where they're old and worn out. It's about mosquitoes." And she recited:

"I see the lights of the village
  Gleam through the rain and the mist,
And a strange foreboding comes o'er me
  That makes me scratch my wrist.

A feeling of doubt and discomfort
  That I cannot quite restrain,
And resembles terror only
  As an itch resembles a pain.

For the dark will be filled with the music
  Of the gnats that infest the night
Till they fold their wings on my forehead
  And silently start to bite."

Freddy was glad he had his hat and whiskers on so that Mrs. Peppercorn couldn't see his expression. But he said: "Excellent! Very good! I have only one criticism. The last lines could come closer to the original, which I believe are 'Shall fold their tents like the Arabs, And silently steal away.' Let me see. Forehead . . .

Arabs— Ah, I have it. 'Till they fold their wings on my spareribs, and silently start to bite.' ''

Mrs. Peppercorn gave a cackle of laughter. "Spar'ibs and Arabs, eh? That's good. Why don't we work together on some of these poems? The one about the village blacksmith, for instance. And by the way, why did Longfellow call him 'Smithy,' do you suppose?''

"Did he?" Freddy asked.

"Of course. 'Under the spreading chestnut tree the village Smithy stands.' ''

"Oh," said Freddy, " 'smithy' is just the old-fashioned name for blacksmith's shop.''

"And there aren't any chestnut trees any more," Mrs. Peppercorn went on. "I shortened it some—like this:

> *Under the spreading maple tree*
> *The blacksmith shoppe stands.*
> *The Smith, a mighty man is he*
> *With hands like iron hams;*
> *And the muscles on his brawny arms*
> *Are big as Superman's.*

Don't you like that better?''

Freddy didn't have to answer, for just then the doorbell rang. It was Mr. Boomschmidt. Mrs. Peppercorn brought him upstairs, and as soon as he was inside the door he said: "Freddy, I bet you're going to be awful mad at

me. I've done something foolish. Oh, my goodness, how mad you're going to be!"

"Well, I can't be mad unless you give me a
chance to," Freddy said.

"Am I going to be mad too?" Mrs. Peppercorn asked. "Because if so, I'll stay. I haven't
been mad at anybody in a week."

"I expect you will, ma'am; I expect you will,"
said Mr. Boomschmidt. "Not that what I did
will injure you personally, but it will injure my
friend Freddy, here, and since you are a friend
of Freddy's, and also, I hope, of mine, I pre-
sume it will injure you—that is, presupposing
your interest in our joint venture in the baseball field, it will—"

"Well, suppose you stop talking and let us
judge," Mrs. Peppercorn interrupted. "What
have you done?"

Mr. Boomschmidt said: "Yes, I suppose I
might as well get down to it. You know,
Freddy, at the end of the fifth inning Kurtz
said to me: 'Looks like you got you a good
team, mister.' 'Yes,' I said, 'I wish now I'd
agreed when you suggested that the winning
team take all of the gate receipts, instead of just
two thirds.'"

"'I guess you'd have had about a thousand
dollars in your pocket,' Kurtz said. 'Understand
that's about what we've taken in.'

"Then he looked at me hard a minute, and he said: 'Tell you what, Boomschmidt,' he said. 'I'm a sport. I'll agree to those terms for the second game. Winner to take all. How about it?'

" 'Why, that hardly seems fair,' I said. 'Looks as if we had this game sewed up now, and my goodness,' I said, 'if we do as well next time you wouldn't get anything.'

"Well, he got kind of unpleasant about it then. Of course if I was scared, he said, we'd let it ride. 'Didn't think you were so timid, Boom,' he said.

"I said, 'I don't like betting on a sure thing, that's all.'

"But he kept on like that, and finally I said: 'All right, Kurtz. If you want to throw money away, I won't stop you, as long as you're throwing it into my pocket.'

"So he wrote on a piece of paper that he agreed that in the second Mars–Tushville game, the winner should get all the gate receipts. I wrote one too, and signed it. Here's his paper, Freddy. And—oh, my gracious, now it looks as if Tushville was going to win both games."

"Oh, don't worry about that," said Freddy. And he tried to console Mr. Boomschmidt. Their third of the first game would pay all the

How will you get that elephant into a uniform?

expenses of both. If Tushville got a thousand dollars from the second one—well, the Martian team hadn't lost any money. "It just means that the team will have to go without uniforms a while longer."

"I know," said Mr. Boomschmidt. "But when we go on the road and get games with other teams, our team will look funny without uniforms."

"So will they look funny *with* uniforms," said Mrs. Peppercorn. "Land sakes, you dress up those spider boys in caps and pants, and shirts with four sleeves—and how you going to get that elephant into a uniform? Why, it'll take fifty yards of cloth."

"When was it that Kurtz made you that proposition?" Freddy asked. "Wasn't it just after Anderson came down out of the grandstand to talk to him?"

"I think so. At the end of the fifth."

"I know what happened," Freddy said. "Anderson has got Squeak-squeak locked up somewhere. And he can make the Martians do anything he wants them to do. They don't dare refuse, because if they do, he might kill Squeak-squeak. I saw him talking to Two-clicks. I'll bet anything that what he said was: 'If you boys ever want to see Squeak-squeak alive again, you do as I say—you swing at every ball that is pitched to you.' "

"I believe you're right, Freddy," said Mr. Boomschmidt. "Oh, my goodness gracious, what a deep-dyed wretch that Anderson is! I suppose he told Kurtz that he could pay the Martians to throw the game. What can we do, Freddy?"

"What I can't understand," Freddy said, "is how he would dare to make such a proposition to Kurtz, who for all he knows is an honest man. He must know Kurtz. Must know he's a crook. Hey, wait a minute! Mr. Boom, let me see how Kurtz signed that paper he gave you."

Mr. Boomschmidt took it from his pocket. "Here it is. J. H. Kurtz. Why, Freddy?"

"Because Anderson turned Squeak-squeak over to someone he called 'Herb.' At least, we're pretty sure he did. Do you suppose that *H* could possibly stand for Herbert? Golly, why did I just look in Centerboro for Herbs? Tushville never occurred to me."

They hurried downstairs to look in the phone book. "J. H. Kurtz," said Mr. Boomschmidt. "That's all it says. Tushville 237. Well, let's find out." And he gave the operator the number.

After a moment Mr. Kurtz's voice answered. "Is this you, Herb?" asked Mr. Boomschmidt.

"Yes. Who's this?" Mr. Kurtz demanded.

It suddenly occurred to Mr. Boomschmidt that, while he'd found out what he wanted to know, he didn't know what to say next. He covered the transmitter with his hand and threw an appealing look over his shoulder at the others.

Freddy didn't know what to say either. But he had a theory that had been very successful in his detective work: when you don't know what to do, do the first thing that comes into your head—the crazier the better. For if you stir things up, something useful is likely to come to the top. And at the worst, you thoroughly confuse the enemy.

So he pushed Mr. Boomschmidt's hand aside, and leaning forward, said into the transmitter: "Help, Herb! Help!" and ended up with a hoarse and terrible screech, before dropping the instrument with a crash onto its cradle. "There," he said. "That ought to unsettle him some."

CHAPTER 17

If the mysterious "Herb" to whom Mr. Anderson had spoken over the phone was really Mr. Kurtz, then it was certain that he would have to be investigated, and quickly. Freddy got in touch with Mr. J. J. Pomeroy, who at once alerted the A.B.I. Early next morning they had set up their headquarters in an abandoned mill on the outskirts of Tushville, and Mr. Kurtz was already under observation. Bumblebees were buzzing around his windows, wasps and beetles and lesser bugs were searching for cracks and crevices through which they might get into his house, and Mrs. Pomeroy was directing local operations from the top of the chimney.

Freddy had wanted to go to Tushville, to be near the field of action, but he felt that he shouldn't go either as himself or as Mr. Arquebus. He decided to sleep on it. He was sleepy anyway, "and when I'm as sleepy as this," he said, "I ought not to make important decisions."

Mrs. Peppercorn had gone downtown after breakfast, and Freddy was sitting on the porch, when Mr. Anderson came up the walk. Freddy didn't have time to retreat; he hardly had time to be scared, before Mr. Anderson was standing over him. But the man seemed to be in a good mood. "Well, Arquebus," he said, "you're certainly a slick operator. You sure had me fooled. Not that I believed in that hick talk, and those phony whiskers. But I didn't guess that you were onto my racket, nor that you were out to hijack any of my stuff. It was just luck I searched your room. I was looking for something else."

"Looking for that 'ere wallet of mine, I expect," said Freddy. "There wasn't no wallet, mister."

"You don't have to talk bad English to me any more, Arquebus," said the other. "I think you and me can do business together. I got a proposition to make you." He dropped into a chair. "Look," he said. "I don't know what you're doing hiding out in a little country town like this; I don't know and I don't ask why you're posing as a baseball coach, nor how you got the job with old Boomschmidt. I won't even ask how you knew I had that stuff in my safe. But that was a slick job, opening that safe. I need someone like you. Look, Henry." He leaned forward and tapped Freddy impressively on the knee. "I've got a secret way of getting into any house in the country. I can get in, and I can get out, without anybody seeing me or knowing anything about it. Furthermore, I can get into a house in, say, Cleveland, and if anybody should see me there, I can prove that I was here in Centerboro within five minutes of the time at which they claim they saw me. I have a perfect alibi. And I can do the same thing for you.

"Now let's get down to cases. Up in Rochester there's a Mrs. Hubert Van Snarll. She's got jewelry that would make that stuff you hijacked out of my safe look like a sockful of broken glass. Only trouble is, she keeps it in a safe in her bedroom, and I ain't any good at safes. I've read books on safe-cracking, and I've taken lessons in it; but it's no good. Last teacher I had, he could drill a little hole in the lock and put some nitroglycerine in and touch it off, and there'd be just a little pop and the door would fly off. But when I tried it—boy, what a bang! The whole building came down on us. They got me out, but I never did see that teacher again."

"But I don't know how to blow open a safe," said Freddy.

"Don't want you to," Mr. Anderson replied. "Job's got to be done quietly. House is full of butlers and housemaids and watchmen and cooks and stuff. That safe, it's the same kind mine is, only it's set in the wall. Anybody that could open mine without knowing the combination won't have any trouble. And there it is, boy, just waiting for us. Fifty-fifty, and the stuff's worth hundreds of thousands. What do you say?"

Freddy had been thinking, and an idea had come to him. It was a terrifying idea, because it meant going burgling with Anderson, and if he was caught in Mr. Van Snarll's bedroom by the butlers and watchmen . . . well, he'd just go to jail. And after he had served his sentence

—what would he get, five years?—he pictured himself, met at the jail door by Jinx and Mrs. Wiggins. Yes, those two he could count on to remain his friends. But how could he face their reproachful looks. And how could he go back and face Mr. Bean? Mr. Bean would probably let him live in his old home, but what would it be like, living there, stripped of his honors, fired from the presidency of the First Animal Bank, shunned by old comrades, snickered at by rabbits. . . .

"Well," said Mr. Anderson impatiently, "what do you say?"

Freddy braced himself. "Sounds all right," he said. "But I'd like to know more before I decide. How do we get there? How do we get in without being caught? How do you happen to know so much about the safe and what's in it?"

"Now, Henry, you just leave all that to me," said Mr. Anderson. "I'll guarantee to get you in and out again without being seen or heard by anyone. As for how I know about the jewelry: I was there the other night—on the roof outside the window—and I saw her put the stuff away But that safe had me licked. Until I found out about you. Well, how about it?"

So after bringing up a few more objections, Freddy agreed to go.

He spent the day in Centerboro, in conference with Leo and Mr. Boomschmidt—and, it must be confessed, in sleep. The reason he gave himself for this was that he would have to be on his toes that night. Of course that was so. But it is also so that while asleep he wasn't scared at the possibility of being arrested as a burglar.

Freddy was lucky that way. His worries never kept him awake. Danger actually made him sleepy. He sometimes wondered if he wouldn't be able to go to sleep right in the middle of a battle.

And of course he was sure that Mr. Pomeroy was quite capable of handling the situation in Tushville. Until something more had been learned as to where Squeak-squeak had been hidden, there wasn't much he could do there.

At ten thirty that evening, as he was sitting in his room, hoping that Mr. Anderson had fallen downstairs and broken his leg—not seriously, but just enough so the Rochester trip would have to be put off—there was a tap at the window. He opened it, and there was Mr. Anderson, beckoning to him from the open door in the turret of the flying saucer, which was hovering so close that he could step right out onto the rim and right into the door.

Besides Freddy and Mr. Anderson, only

Two-clicks, who was driving, was in the saucer.
And Freddy had no time to say anything to the
Martian, for within two minutes, as he looked
out through the window, the lights of Rochester
swept up from the western horizon and spread
out beneath them, and the saucer slackened,
dipped, and swung along slowly at treetop level
to stop within a foot of a third-story back window in a large brick house. Mr. Anderson said
to Two-clicks: "Hover a couple of hundred feet
up. When you see two flashes from this window, come down and pick us up." Then he
stepped out, raised the window, and Freddy followed him in.

The room was a bedroom, furnished but evidently unused. Mr. Anderson explained in a
whisper that the room below was Mrs. Van
Snarll's bedroom. "She's out at a party tonight,
and won't be home before midnight," he said.
"We've got over an hour to go down and get
into that safe."

"And where are all the butlers and housemaids?" Freddy asked.

"The maid has tidied up her room and
turned down her bed. None of 'em will come
up again tonight. Come along."

They went out and down the stairs and into
a bedroom below, guided by Mr. Anderson's
flashlight. There was a dim light burning in

the room, which was luxuriously furnished. Curtains and upholstery were in red damask; the bed was turned down and a red-plush night-gown was laid out on it, and below on the floor was a pair of matching red-plush slippers.

"My goodness, she sure must be rich!" Freddy exclaimed, as he peered around under his glasses. He went over to examine the gold toilet articles on the dressing table.

Mr. Anderson had gone over to a large wall mirror; he took hold of it and pulled, and as it swung away from the wall, Freddy saw the door of the safe behind it.

"All right, boy—go to it," said Mr. Anderson, and stood back, rubbing his hands in anticipation.

Freddy went across and looked at the safe. He spun the dials experimentally a few times, then began feeling in his pockets. First in one, then in another, becoming more and more agitated, until at last he said: "It's gone! I've lost it! I must have dropped it in that there flying machine."

"Must have dropped what?" Mr. Anderson demanded. "You don't need anything but your fingers to open that safe. Come on—get going!"

"That's just it," Freddy said. "My fingers. I always have to sandpaper 'em down a little before I go to work on a safe, so they'll be

In a few seconds the saucer was hovering at the window sill.

sensitive enough for the job. And I lost the sandpaper."

Well, Mr. Anderson had quite a lot to say about Mr. Arquebus's carelessness, and he said it in a savage whisper. But Freddy didn't listen. He was edging toward the door. And just as he reached it, Mr. Anderson said: "Well, wait here and I'll get it. And don't lose your fingers while I'm gone."

But Freddy had the door open, and from outside he said: "I'll get it. I think I know where I dropped it." He was gone before Anderson could say any more.

He guessed rightly that Mr. Anderson wouldn't try to stop him, once he had started. After all, the man had no reason to believe that he would do anything but try to find the sandpaper and come back with it. But Freddy had other ideas. In the third-floor room he went to the window and with his own flashlight flashed twice at the sky. In a few seconds the saucer was hovering at the window sill, and he stepped into the turret.

"Where Andyson?" Two-clicks inquired.

"He stay; we go," said Freddy. And as Two-clicks hesitated: "He say tell you, go quick! He coming bimeby next week on train."

The Martians had naturally found a good deal in earth people's behavior that was impossible to understand. To Two-clicks, this was just another instance of it. He shrugged his four shoulders, slid the turret door shut, and five minutes later Freddy was back at Mrs. Peppercorn's. He went to the telephone, called the operator, and said: "I want to talk to someone in police headquarters in Rochester, New York."

CHAPTER
18

Early the next morning Freddy had another talk with Mr. Boomschmidt, and then Mr. Hercules drove him over to the A.B.I. headquarters on the outskirts of Tushville. The old mill was buzzing with activity. Every minute or two bumblebee couriers were arriving with reports of the latest developments at the Kurtz house, and others were taking off, with instructions as to what should be done next.

A great deal, Mrs. Pomeroy told him, had been accomplished. Squeak-squeak was definitely in the house. There was an old wine cellar back of the regular cellar, which had a heavy wooden door, strongly padlocked. The Martian had been heard talking through this door to Mrs. Kurtz. "Our operatives, however," said Mrs. Pomeroy, "have not yet been able to establish communication with him."

She said that Jacob, the wasp, and a dozen of his relatives were in conference with Mr. Pomeroy; they had proposed a direct attack on the house. They felt that a company of wasps could drive the Kurtzes out of the house. A rescue party of animals could then enter the house and set the Martian free.

But several of the wasps reported that Mrs. Kurtz had a spray gun believed to contain DDT, and that she was uncivilized enough to use it, even against harmless gnats and flies who were only minding their own business. Mr. Pomeroy, therefore, had felt that while the scheme might be successful, the casualty rate would be too high. So he vetoed the plan and the conference broke up.

"Quite right," said Freddy. "We can find some other way, I'm sure."

They were discussing this when a bumble-bee returned with news that Mrs. Kurtz and her cook had had a fight and the cook had left.

"That doesn't help any," said Mr. Pomeroy.

"Perhaps it does," said Freddy. "Just what happened?" he asked the bee.

It seemed that the cook was not very bright and it had taken her a long time to find out that there was a prisoner in the cellar. It wasn't indeed until she got to wondering what became of all the peanuts that Mr. Kurtz brought home, and why it was that he took them down-cellar and always returned empty-handed, that she began to put two and two together. She went down, rapped on the wine-cellar door, and when someone or something returned her rap from the other side, she demanded an explanation.

Well, Mrs. Kurtz said, they were keeping a vicious dog there.

The cook said she never heard of a dog being fed exclusively on peanuts, and anyway it was a crime to lock up an animal that way.

So then Mrs. Kurtz said it was a dangerous criminal they had captured, and they were waiting for the police to come and get him.

The cook said she thought the police were

pretty slow, and she said anyway she didn't like it and she was going to leave. Mrs. Kurtz begged her to stay until she could get somebody else, but the cook said nothing doing, and went.

"H'm," said Freddy. "Ha!" And he put on the Great Detective expression.

Almost immediately he wished he hadn't put it on, for he had got an idea—a dangerous idea —such an idea as a Great Detective would at once put into action, at no matter what risk to himself. And he didn't want to. But with that expression on he had no choice. "Herc," he said, "drive me out to the farm right away."

A little over an hour later he was back in Tushville. But you wouldn't have recognized him. Or, if you did, it would have been more polite not to say so. For he was in disguise. He had on an old gingham dress of Mrs. Bean's, a sunbonnet, and a pair of black mitts, and he carried a shopping bag. Two handsome chestnut curls were pinned into the sunbonnet and hung down on either side of his face.

This disguise was a favorite with Freddy, because when he wore it he pretended to be an old Irishwoman, and he spoke an imitation Irish brogue which he thought very convincing. It wasn't; it was dreadful. But as Freddy didn't know that, and considered it to be the real thing, he sometimes got away with it. It is often the case that if you believe in anything enough, you make other people believe in it too.

Freddy had Mr. Hercules drop him at the corner nearest the Kurtz house, then he walked slowly down and turned in at the gate. He stopped, looking up at the house, took a piece of paper from his pocket and appeared to consult it, then went up the steps and rang the bell

After a minute a big, hard-featured woman came to the door. "Well," she said crossly, "what is it?"

"The top of the mornin' to ye, ma'am," said Freddy. "And do I be speakin' to Mrs. John B. Anguish?"

"No, you do not!" snapped the woman, and slammed the door.

"Dear me," said Freddy, and rang the bell again.

The door flew open. "Say, what's the matter with you?" the woman stormed. "Now get away from this door and stay there!"

She started to slam the door again, but Freddy quickly dropped down into a porch chair, and she came back out and stood threateningly over her visitor. "I said, get away from this door!"

"Ah, sure," said Freddy in a wheedling

"*I said get away from this door!*"

voice, "ye'd not grudge me a bit of rest, ma'am?
I dunno is there a Mrs. Anguish on this block,
and she after hiring me for the cooking and
general housework and then givin' me the
wrong directions for finding her home, the way
I've tramped the livin' legs off me huntin' it—"

"You mean you're a cook?" the woman demanded suddenly. "Come in, come in, I want
to talk to you."

This of course was what Freddy had hoped
for, but he was smart enough to raise some objections, so that he found himself seized by
the arm and forcibly propelled into the house.
He continued to raise objections when Mrs.
Kurtz tried to hire him, and she was so determined to argue them down that half an hour
later he had been engaged as a cook, paid a
week's salary in advance, and given a comfortable room on the second floor—all without even
being asked for his references.

Freddy's career as a cook lasted only five
days, and they were not happy ones. The very
first dinner he served to the Kurtzes was anything but a success: the steak had been cooked
until it was about as easy to chew as the side
of an old boot, while the potatoes were raw. As
for the pie, the less said the better.

"Throw this stuff out," Mrs. Kurtz said angrily. "I thought you said you were a cook!"

Mr. Kurtz was feeling his jaw. "I bent all my front teeth trying to bite into that pie," he complained.

"Ah, well now, and maybe it was a bit too well done," said Freddy. "'Tis O'Halloran—me late lamented—you'd best be blamin' for that. 'Ye cook things too soft, Bridie,' he'd say. 'I like somethin' I can get me teeth into.' But sure 'tis a terrible thing to bend a tooth. I remember—"

"We're not interested in your reminiscences," said Mrs. Kurtz. "Take that sunbonnet off and go on back and wash the dishes. Come along, Herb, we'll go down and get something to eat at the lunchroom."

"Sure, 'tis sorry I am you'll not be likin' the good vittles," Freddy said. "But tomorry I'll make ye a shepherd's pie—"

"I suppose you'd put the shepherd in, boots and all," said Mrs. Kurtz sarcastically. "Well I'll take care of the cooking from now on."

"You're givin' me notice, ma'am?"

Mrs. Kurtz frowned. "No," she said thoughtfully. "No. I've got to have someone for the housework. If you want to stay on till I can find someone that can cook, you can do so. Can you scrub? Without going through the floor?"

"Can I scrub, is it? You'll not find the like of Bridget O'Halloran for scrubbing between here and the fifth of next March. Sure, show me the floor ye want scrubbed, and if it's twice as dirty as Barney's pig, I'll scrub it as white as snow."

So Mrs. Kurtz gave him a brush and a pail and set him to work, and she and Mr. Kurtz went off down to the lunchroom.

As soon as they were out of the door Freddy hurried down-cellar. He found the door to the wine cellar. There was a sort of hatch about six inches square in the heavy door, and Freddy slid it aside and said: "Squeak-squeak, are you there? This is Freddy. Are you all right?"

The Martian was so excited to hear a familiar voice that at first Freddy couldn't understand what he said, but pretty soon he calmed down. He was all right, he said, but very sick of peanuts and water, which was all he had had to eat since he had been kidnapped. He was also sick of sitting on the floor in the dark. Had Freddy come to get him out?

Freddy said he had but he didn't know yet how. And he was trying to reassure the Martian when they heard footsteps upstairs and realized that the Kurtzes had come back.

Freddy dashed up into the kitchen and dropped to his knees and resumed his scrubbing. Why had they come back so soon? They hadn't had time to eat dinner. Did they suspect something? Then he found that they had bought sandwiches, and Mrs. Kurtz made some coffee and they sat down in the kitchen and ate, and watched Freddy scrub. Evidently they intended to keep an eye on him.

Indeed they kept so close an eye on him that for the next three days he was not given a chance to get down-cellar unobserved. Mrs. Kurtz kept him scrubbing and housecleaning and washing curtains and vacuuming rugs from the time he got up until it was time for bed. If he had really been Mrs. O'Halloran he would have walked out after the first day. But he felt that his only chance to release Squeak-squeak was to stick to the job.

It was on Friday—the day before the Mars–Tushville game—that Freddy decided that he would really have to take some action if Squeak-squeak was to be rescued in time to win. For unless he was free, the Martians would throw the game. They wouldn't have any choice.

He had kept in touch with his friends through Mr. Pomeroy, who came to his window every evening. And that evening he told the robin to round up the wasps and have them stand by in A.B.I. headquarters at the old mill. "I managed today," he said, "to empty all the DDT out of the spray gun and the bottle, and

I refilled them with water. Now when we attack, the only damage will be a few wet wings."

"You really think this will work?" said Mr. Pomeroy. "You think a few stings will make Kurtz hand over the wine-cellar key?"

"It won't be a few, it'll be a lot," Freddy said. "And I don't say the plan is perfect. It's the only one I can think of. I think you'd better have some reserves handy. Leo and Mrs. Wiggins and Jinx and anybody else that will volunteer. We just might have to make a general attack in force, and we want to have the force where we can call on it. The wasps attack tomorrow morning at dawn. I've found that the Kurtzes are pretty dopey before breakfast."

Next morning, just as the light began to grow in the east, Freddy unhooked the screen at his window, and Jacob and his family, with some twenty other wasps who had come along for the fun, flew in and lined up on the footboard of the bed. All the wasps wore an expression of pleased anticipation. It is considered bad manners for a wasp to sting anyone without provocation, although it is sometimes done out of sheer high spirits. But they enjoy using their stings; they like to see people jump; and to be asked to sting humans in a good cause was an unusual and delightful opportunity.

Freddy explained that what he wanted to get

was the key to Squeak-squeak's dungeon. "I'll open the Kurtzes' bedroom door as quietly as I can and you'll all go in. Then when I've got the key out and locked the door from the outside, you boys can give 'em a few stings to wake 'em up. Don't sting 'em any more after that; it'll be enough if they find themselves shut in a room with a lot of wasps flying around and making passes at 'em. Then I'll call to 'em from outside and tell 'em I'll let 'em out if they'll give up the key."

"O.K.," said Jacob. "But once they get started, I don't know if I can hold my boys back. They're going to want one sting apiece, anyway."

"I'm sorry," said Freddy firmly, "but that's just out. These people are crooks, but I just want to get the key—I don't want to send 'em to the hospital."

"Well," said Jacob, "I'll do my best."

The first part of Freddy's scheme worked perfectly. He tiptoed down the hall, opened the Kurtzes' bedroom door, and quietly changed the key from the inside to the outside of the lock. A loud and not unmusical duet of snores came from the darkness. "Boy, will they sing a different tune in just a minute!" Jacob whispered. Then as the wasps filed in, Freddy closed and locked the door. And the fun began.

The duet broke off in a series of sharp yelps; then there was the double thump of feet hitting the floor; the doorknob rattled, and Mrs. Kurtz's voice shrieked: "Herb, you fool, you locked the door—we can't get out!" Then there were some more yelps.

Freddy banged on the door. "Lay off a minute, Jacob," he called. Then: "Mr. Kurtz, 'tis me thrained wasps I've set on ye, and I'll not be callin' 'em off until I have the key to the wine cellar in me hand. Sure, it's ate up entirely you'll be, for it's determined I am to rescue the poor creature is your prisoner. So do ye hand me the key, sorr, or do I set the wasps on again, the way ye'll be covered with bumps like an ould potato?"

"Open the door," Mr. Kurtz groaned. "I'll give you the key."

So Freddy unlocked the door and pushed it open a crack. At the same moment it was violently pulled away from him from inside; he was yanked forward and fell into the room. Then he saw stars as something hit him on the head, and he passed out.

When he came to a few minutes later, a small voice said in his ear: "Are you all right, Freddy?" It was Jacob. A number of the wasps, perched on the rim of the sunbonnet, were fanning him with their wings.

Freddy sat up. He had a headache, and when he felt of his head, there was a good-sized lump on it, but the sunbonnet had protected him from a more serious wound. "The Kurtzes—did they get away?" he asked.

"They got as far as the cellar," said the wasp. "They've locked themselves in there. Boy, we had some fun with them! They made a break for that sprayer first. They were going to have themselves a time, knocking us out with DDT. And were they surprised when we flew right through the spray and stuck 'em! I got old Kurtz in the back of the neck—my favorite place. They yell louder when they get it there than any other spot. Must be specially sensitive."

Freddy got up. "We mustn't let 'em get out of the cellar," he said. "Keep 'em in a state of siege. Any of your boys in there with them?"

"No. They were too quick for us. Got through the door to the cellar stairs and locked it before we knew what they were up to. But we've posted sentries at the cellar windows. They can't get out without getting some more doses of the poison."

"Well," Freddy said, "we can probably starve 'em out."

"Before this afternoon?" said Jacob. "The game starts in just a few hours."

"Well," said Freddy thoughtfully, "they haven't had any breakfast yet." And he went down into the kitchen and made coffee and fried a lot of bacon. "Let's see what happens when they smell that," he said.

CHAPTER 19

The appetizing smells of fresh coffee and frizzling bacon filled the kitchen. They seeped through the cracks round the cellar door and rolled down the stairs and up the noses of Mr. and Mrs. Kurtz. And pretty soon Mr. Kurtz came up and rapped on the door.

"Yes?" said Freddy.

"We want to make a deal with you," Mr. Kurtz said.

"I'll not make any deals," Freddy said. "You send that Martian up into the kitchen, and I'll clear out and take the wasps with me."

"Look, Mrs. O'Halloran," said Mr. Kurtz, "what's it worth to you to just go away and forget all about this Martian you're talking about? I can promise you a lot of money—how about a thousand dollars?"

"Where you going to get it—from Anderson? Anderson's in jail," said Freddy.

As a matter of fact Mr. Anderson, who, on the tip Freddy had phoned to the Rochester police, had been arrested, was again at liberty. Although he had been caught burglarizing Mrs. Van Snarll's house, there was no proof that he was implicated in the other recent burglaries. That he had had a hand in them seemed pretty certain, and it seemed to the authorities more important to locate the stolen jewelry than to keep him in jail. So they had let him out on bail and had asked the state troopers in Tushville to keep an eye on him.

Mr. Kurtz was silent for a minute, evidently surprised that Mrs. O'Halloran should know about his tie-up with Anderson, which he had supposed well hidden. Then he said: "I'll give you two thousand. That's as far as I can go."

It was just then that Jinx came into the kitchen. He jerked his head at Freddy to come away from the cellar door. "Mr. Boom's down at the mill," he said in a low tone. "And he's getting worried. Gosh, Freddy, it's only about four hours till the game starts." He stared at the pig and grinned. "Gosh, you certainly look cute in that bonnet."

"I don't know what to do, Jinx, and that's the truth," Freddy said, and he told the cat what had happened. "I'd have sent J.J. for the elephants and Mrs. Wiggins and some of the bigger animals earlier, but I don't believe even Hannibal could break down that wine-closet door. The wood's four inches thick, and it's bound with iron. I figured the wasps were a better bet. But now we're stuck."

A wasp buzzed in the window and lit on Freddy's bonnet. "Anderson's coming up the front walk," he said. "Shall we chase him off?"

"No. Let's see what he wants. Jinx, curl up in that chair and try to look at home."

A moment later the doorbell rang. Freddy went to the door. Mr. Anderson put down a large suitcase and took off his hat politely. "Good morning, ma'am. Is Mr. Kurtz at home?"

"Ah, it's sorry he will be to miss you, sir," Freddy said. "He's just stepped down to the school—"

At that moment from behind the cellar door came Mr. Kurtz's voice. "She's lying, Anderson. Help! They've got me locked down-cellar. Get the troopers."

Mr. Anderson started toward the kitchen. "What's going on here?" he demanded.

"Show him, Jacob," said Freddy, and the wasps swarmed to the attack.

Mr. Anderson made one bound to the front door. He snatched up his suitcase and the second bound carried him down the steps and halfway to the gate. And with each bound he yelled. But Freddy called the wasps back. "It's no good," he said. "Let's wait for the troopers."

Freddy had been surprised to see Mr. Anderson. But he guessed why he had been released from jail. He didn't think Anderson would come with the troopers—probably he would phone them. And indeed that was what happened. The troopers got there in about fifteen minutes. Freddy was sitting in a rocking chair by the window.

"Now, ma'am," said the taller trooper, "what's this all about? We got a report the Kurtzes are locked in the cellar."

"Sure, they're locked in, but the key's on

their side," Freddy said. "Nobody's keeping them there."

"Who are you?" the trooper demanded.

"Bridget O'Halloran, at your service," said Freddy. "Sure, I'm new in this place but I'll not be here long. It's ravin' lunatics these Kurtzes are, officer. I was hired as a cook, not as a keeper. Runnin' up and down and screech-in' that bugs are bitin' them, and offerin' me diamond necklaces if I'd keep still about the prisoner is locked up in the wine cellar—"

"Diamond necklaces?" The trooper looked interested.

At this moment the cellar door opened and Mr. Kurtz poked out his head. Seeing no wasps, he came out into the kitchen. "Arrest that woman, officer," he demanded. "Certainly I've got a prisoner in the cellar. He's this woman's accomplice. I caught them in my bed-room last night. I captured him, but she drove us down-cellar again at the point of a gun."

" 'Tis a howlin' great liar ye are, Kurtz, surely," said Freddy. "Ask him about the dia-mond necklace that him and Anderson, over at Centerboro, stole. Then go down and look at his prisoner. Why is he keeping one of them Martians from the circus locked up, and them to be playing ball against his own team this day?"

The troopers looked at each other, and the smaller one said: "Let's get this prisoner up and have a look at him."

So he got the key from Mr. Kurtz and went down-cellar, and a minute later came up with Squeak-squeak.

The tall trooper said: "I guess we'd better take the whole lot in, and let the judge sort 'em out. I can't make any sense out of it."

"We haven't got any place to keep prisoners," said the short trooper. "Unless one of us stays there this afternoon to keep an eye on 'em. And I want to go to that game over in Centerboro. You do too, I guess."

"So does the judge," said the other.

"Sure. The judge won't thank us to bring these folks up before him now. Tell you what, Joe; let's lock 'em in that wine cellar. After the game we can pick 'em up and take 'em down to headquarters for the night."

Freddy and the Kurtzes all began protesting at once, but it did them no good. Five minutes later they were locked in the wine cellar, sitting on kitchen chairs which the troopers had thoughtfully provided. But Jinx and the wasps —except half a dozen who stayed with Freddy to keep the Kurtzes in order—set out for the mill, to tell Mr. Pomeroy and Mr. Boomschmidt what had happened.

At the mill, as soon as they arrived, things began to move; Mr. Pomeroy set out at top speed for Centerboro, with instructions to delay the game as much as possible. Mr. Boomschmidt hopped in his car, and after stopping to buy some tools at the Tushville hardware store, drove straight to the Kurtzes'.

By a quarter to two that afternoon a huge crowd filled the grandstand and the bleachers, and overflowed the grounds at the Centerboro ball park. Most of them were unaware that several of the most important figures in the afternoon's program were not present; and it wasn't until the two teams came out and started to warm up that the absence of the Martian coach, and the distinguished third baseman, Mr. Boomschmidt, was noted.

Henrietta, as usual leading the cheering section, noticed it first, and she soon had the Bean animals and the circus contingent chanting: "We want Arquebus! We want Boomschmidt!" But as neither of these gentlemen responded, Leo, who had had word from Mr. Pomeroy, stepped out and announced that there would be a slight delay; Mr. Boomschmidt, Mr. Arquebus, and Mr. Kurtz would be along soon. In the meantime, the circus quartet would oblige with a song.

So then Mr. Hercules and Leo and Uncle

They all had deep bass voices.

Bill, the buffalo, and Andrew, the hippopotamus, came out and put their arms about one another's shoulders, and sang "Rocked in the Cradle of the Deep." They all had deep bass voices, and when Andrew went way down on the last "deep," the people in the stands glanced apprehensively over their shoulders at the sky. It was certainly more like a distant thunderstorm than a song.

But after the quartet had sung six numbers, the audience began to get restless, and began stamping its feet and yelling: "Come on! Play ball!"

So Leo went out again and introduced Mr. Hercules, who did some weight-lifting and juggled cannonballs. But this didn't keep the people quiet much longer either, and the rougher element began throwing pop bottles at Leo. And Black Beard, the Tushville captain, said: "Get your team out here, or I'm going to claim this game by default."

Mr. Pomeroy had told the Martians what had happened at the Kurtz house in Tushville, and that Squeak-squeak was found and would soon be at liberty. He urged them therefore to disregard Mr. Anderson's threats and to follow Mr. Arquebus's orders. "I tell you, Squeak-squeak is safe!" he insisted.

But they were not convinced. "We 'fraid for

Squeak-squeak," Two-clicks said. "You bring Squeak-squeak here, we play like Mr. Arky say —oh, very good."

"We've got to start the game," the robin said to Leo. "And they're going to throw it; they're going to swing at everything. We'll just have to go as slowly as possible, and hope that Mr. Boom will get Squeak-squeak here in time. And just look over there." Mr. Anderson, with a big suitcase in his hand, was standing by the corner of the grandstand. As they looked, they saw him motion to Two-clicks, who went over to him. Anderson said something, and the Martian nodded agreement gloomily.

So with one of the alligators in Mr. Boom-schmidt's place at third base, the game started.

CHAPTER
20

The first inning did not go so badly. Black Beard struck out, Smith singled but was caught trying to steal second, and Swiggett hit a high fly to Mr. Hercules. For the Martians, Hannibal singled but got to second on a fumble, Oscar surprisingly hit a two bagger and brought the elephant in, but tripped and fell over his feet and was tagged out trying to steal third. The alligator, never a strong hitter, hit one into the first baseman's hands. And then Chirp-squeak came up. He swung at everything and was out.

In the second Tushville got three runs, largely owing to the jitters that had come over the Martian team. The four Martians were of course useless; if they played well and won the game, Mr. Anderson had threatened that they would never see Squeak-squeak again. And the others, realizing this, were too worried to play well. Except Oscar, of course, who hadn't brains enough to worry. And when Mars came to bat, Chirp, Click-two-squeaks and Two-clicks fanned out in that order.

By this time everybody in the stands knew that Mars was going to lose. It was perfectly plain that as long as the Martians swung at everything they would strike out. And the others weren't strong enough to make up for it. Mr. Hercules and Leo and Hannibal were hitters, and played their positions well. But Oscar was uneven, and the alligator was a weak hitter and hadn't much of a throwing arm.

By the end of the sixth the score was Tushville 11, Mars 1, and Leo was in despair. "What can we do, Hannibal?" he said. "Where *is* the chief? He's had enough time to bust them out of that wine cellar, hasn't he? And where's J.J.? *He's* gone now!"

Through it all Chirp-squeak pitched to the best of his ability. The crowd in the stands seemed to recognize this, for they jeered at the other Martians, but not at him. Even the Tushville rooters groaned when the Martians continued swinging at balls that were a foot out of their reach. And Mr. Anderson, in his front-row seat, wore a wide and happy grin.

And then Mr. Pomeroy came flying at top speed, banked sharply, and lit on Leo's head. "They're coming!" he panted. "Mr. Boom sawed a hole in the door. My gosh—what a job!—it's four inches thick. Took nearly three hours."

All at once Mr. Boomschmidt's big red car, with the Boomschmidt coat of arms on the door panels, came into the ball park, swept around in a half-circle and drew up in front of the grandstand. And out climbed Squeak-squeak and Jinx and the Kurtzes and Mr. Boomschmidt. And Mr. Arquebus. For the beard and the wig and the Prince Albert coat and the hat and the spectacles had been in Mrs. O'Halloran's shopping bag, and Freddy had changed into them on the road.

Well, the stands cheered and cheered, and

Henrietta turned so many somersaults that she became quite dizzy and had to be laid down on the grass and have smelling salts held under her nose. The Martians were wild with delight at having Squeak-squeak back safe. But after a word with Mr. Kurtz, Mr. Anderson went quietly out to his car and drove off, taking his suitcase with him.

Then Leo told Mr. Boomschmidt and Freddy what the score was.

"Well, come on then," Freddy shouted. "What is this—beginning of the seventh? We've got a chance. Come on, boys; for home, for Boomschmidt, and for Bean! Let's show these Tushvillains how us Martians play baseball!"

But as the team started out to take up positions, Mr. Boomschmidt said: "Oh, my goodness, Freddy, I'm all worn out. I sawed on that old door for three hours straight. I don't believe I can play. If somebody threw a ball at me I'd fall down flat. Look, Freddy, why don't you take my place at third?"

"Why, I never played baseball in my life," Freddy said.

"You coached, though."

"There's nobody else but that alligator," said Leo. "Come on, pig; give it a try."

"In this outfit—in these glasses?" Freddy protested. And then it occurred to him that, with

He snatched off hat, coat, whiskers, and glasses and ran out to third base.

Squeak-squeak back, it wasn't necessary for him to be Mr. Arquebus any more. So he snatched off hat, coat, whiskers, and glasses, grabbed the glove from Mr. Boomschmidt, and ran out to third base. And when the people in the stands saw who Mr. Arquebus really was, they all jumped up and waved their hats and yelled themselves hoarse. And Mrs. Bean, in her front-row seat, yelled louder than anybody.

From then on the Martians played magnificently. They had to; for to overtake a lead of ten runs was almost impossible. In the seventh inning Tushville didn't get a hit, while Mr. Hercules' home run brought in three Martians, who by refusing to swing at anything, had got their bases on balls. This made the score Tushville 11, Mars 5.

The eighth inning was much like the seventh, except that when Oscar went after a pop-up hit by Oigle, he tried to show off by catching it in his beak, and swallowed the ball. He just stood there, looking foolish, while the bulge made by the ball went slowly down his long neck, and the stands rocked with laughter. So Mr. Boomschmidt took him out and made him go lie down, while Squeak-squeak went in at shortstop.

At the beginning of the ninth the score was Tushville 11, Mars 9. Tushville was shut out in the first half, which put it up to Mars to pile up three more runs in the second half if they were to win.

The first man up to bat was Squeak-squeak, taking Oscar's place. Squeak-squeak was a little smaller than the other Martians, and therefore even harder to pitch to. He just stood there and watched the four balls go by, and then trotted to first.

Freddy came next. He stood at the plate, watching Smith wind up before delivering the pitch, when something flashed in his eyes, blinding him. He didn't even see the ball, but he heard it smack in the catcher's mitt. "Strike!" called the umpire.

Again Freddy stood up to the plate, and again the light flashed just before Smith threw. This time the umpire called a ball.

Freddy stood back from the plate. "Somebody down by the fence is flashing a mirror in my eyes," he called to Mr. Boomschmidt, who sat on the bench.

Mr. Boomschmidt got up and went over to speak to the two troopers who were standing at the end of the grandstand, pretending not to see their recent prisoners so that they wouldn't have to arrest them again and miss the rest of the game. One of the men—the one with the motorcycle, jumped on his machine, kicked it into life, and cut off across the diamond to where, by the left-field fence, Mr. Anderson was standing with a pocket mirror in his hand.

Just what happened then Freddy could not see at that distance. But evidently Mr. Anderson hit the trooper, for he was sprawling on his back, and Mr. Anderson, astride the motorcycle with the big suitcase across the handlebars, was roaring back across the diamond. The only exit from the ball park was through the gate by the grandstand, and before anybody could move to stop him—if they could have stopped him—Anderson shot through the gate.

It was then that Mr. Hercules acted. He picked up a baseball, and as Anderson shot past him he began to wind up for a pitch. By the time he threw, Anderson was about the same distance a batter would have been from a pitcher. Nobody expected the ball to hit Anderson, or to do much harm if it did, for by this time he was going nearly fifty miles an hour.

But a fast pitch can travel nearly a hundred miles an hour, and Mr. Hercules had a very fast ball. The ball overtook Anderson at something like fifty miles an hour, struck him fairly between the shoulders, and knocked him neatly off the machine, which went on for nearly a hundred feet before tipping over and throwing off the suitcase, which burst open and spilled a flashing cascade of jewelry over the grass.

The stands were in an uproar. The crowd was on its feet, yelling, as the second trooper ran out of the gate and handcuffed Mr. Anderson, who was apparently dazed, but not seriously hurt, by his fall. After he was led away, and the jewelry was repacked in the suitcase and stowed in the trooper's car, the excitement died down. Mr. Boomschmidt signaled to Henrietta, who was now on her feet again, and she ran out in front of the cheering section and called for a Martian cheer for Squeak-squeak— the one with the Martian "hurrah" in it. After that there was a sneezing cheer for Mr. Boomschmidt, and then she made up a special cheer for Freddy, ending: "piggy-wiggy-wiggy! Oink, oink, oink!" Freddy didn't like it very much.

Then the game went on. Freddy watched Smith wind up for the pitch, he saw his arm come forward and his hand release the ball, which came toward him at what seemed like tremendous speed. This was the first fast ball Freddy had ever had to stand up to, for the mirror flashing in his eyes had blinded him to the other two. It scared him. He ducked and put up the bat, not to hit the ball, but to protect himself from it. And there was a crack!

and he felt his hands tingle. And then he looked and saw the ball sailing out just over the shortstop's head.

For a second he stood there looking at it in amazement, then Mr. Boomschmidt's voice shouted: "Run, Freddy! My goodness gracious, don't stand there! Run!"

So Freddy ran. As he rounded first, his old enemy, Black Beard, deliberately put out a foot and tried to trip him. But Freddy saw it in time. He dropped to all fours and plowed right through the man, tossing him in the air to come down with a thud that knocked the wind out of him. Then he got to third before the right fielder got the ball back to the third baseman. That brought Squeak-squeak in, and the score was now 11 to 10.

Chirp-squeak and Chirp got their base on balls, then Click-two-squeaks walked, forcing Freddy in and tying the score. The Tushville pitcher was game. He stuck to his guns, and using every ounce of skill he had, he managed to get two strikes on Two-clicks. But he couldn't keep it up. After that he pitched four straight balls, Chirp-squeak was forced in, and the game was won, 12 to 11.

After they had been cheered and shaken hands with and congratulated by what seemed to Freddy everyone in the ball park, he and

Jinx and Leo slipped away from the crowd as it streamed out of the gates.

"It's nice we won the game and the team will have its uniforms," said the pig, "but I'm glad all this business is over. My goodness, I'd like a little peace and quiet."

"I don't know what you're kicking about," said Jinx. "You started the whole business—the Martian baseball team and all. And a couple of your old enemies—Kurtz and Anderson—have been hauled off to the hoosegow. Not to speak of the reward for finding all that jewelry, which you'll get part of anyway."

"Oh, sure; I know all that," said Freddy. "But there's been too much going on. I miss the barnyard, the long quiet evenings in the pig pen, working at my poetry. I miss the animals. I've had too much to do with people—humans, I mean. Oh, I don't mean the Beans, and Mr. Boom, and the circus people. But all these mobs. Look at 'em." He waved an arm at the crowds filing out of the gate.

"You're getting to be a snob like Oscar, only the other way round," said Leo. "There was a couple of years when he wouldn't speak to anybody that had more than two legs. You're going to stick up your nose at anybody that has less than four. Next thing, you'll be taking off your hat to centipedes."

"Oh, it isn't that," Freddy protested. "It's just that I've been with humans so much lately that they begin to look funny to me. Look at that boy with his mouth open. A horse or a cow doesn't look silly like that. Look at that woman with the hat with pink flowers all over it. You never see a pig wearing a monstrosity like that."

"Oh, I don't know," said the cat. "Might be right becoming to you. Like that sunbonnet. Hide your face, anyway."

But Freddy just grinned. "I started a piece about how funny people look compared to animals," he said. "It goes like this:

> *Oh, why do people go to zoos*
> *To see giraffes and kangaroos,*
> *When creatures just as odd may be*
> *Observed among the bourgeoisie?*"

"Among the which?" Jinx asked.

"Bourgeoisie," said the pig. "That means just —well, people. Like that crowd there."

"Children too?" Leo asked.

"Children mostly," said Freddy. "We'll come to them." And he went on:

> *"I often wonder why giraffes*
> *Are only rated good for laughs,*
> *When they're so dignified and loyal.*
> *It sometimes makes me really boil.*

By some, the hippopotamus
Is thought a quite odd-looking cuss
And at him, kids who're impolite
Will smile, or even laugh outright.

Even the pig does not escape
From every kind of jeer and jape.
His air of calm and sterling worth
Does not protect from vulgar mirth.

Yet people should provoke your smiles
Much oftener than animiles
And as for children—goodness me,
How curious looking can you be?

For though by mothers deemed a blessing
To look at, they are quite distressing.
The toad, to look at, is no joy
But is he funnier than a boy?

The aardvark makes your senses whirl,
But he's no curiouser than a girl.
To me, quite frankly, it's bewilderin'
How folks can get so fond of children."

"That covers that, I think," remarked Leo.
"Not quite," said Freddy.

*"Had I my way, I'd put the skids
Under the whole darned race of kids,"*

Jinx said dreamily.

"You take a slightly more comprehensive view than I do," said Leo. "On the whole, I agree. Particularly when I think of the years I've spent in a cage, having my tail pulled and paper bags burst in my ears and things thrown at me. But I remember what my Uncle Ajax used to say. 'Children,' he said, 'are not strictly speaking animals at all. They're not grown-ups, either. More like some kind of very active bug. A bug with a habit of making loud noises that don't mean anything. But you can get along with them if you can forget how funny they look, and if you remember to treat them as if they had a lot of sense. That, of course,' Uncle Ajax said, 'is important in dealing with grown-ups too. In fact,' he said, 'although in theory kids and grown-ups are different species, in practice there ain't enough difference between 'em to fill the hole in a doughnut.' "

"Do you mind if I make use of some of your Uncle Ajax's wisdom in completing this poem?" Freddy asked.

"Not at all," said the lion. "Only—look, Freddy, I've got an idea. Let's write a book on good manners. We're agreed, aren't we, that animals have better manners than humans? You never see a cow, for instance, eating with her knife. You never see a rabbit wearing his hat in the house. Well, why isn't that important? Why shouldn't we point out the things that are bad manners, and at the same time show that animals don't do them?"

"Not a bad idea," said Freddy. "Book like that would have a big sale among animals. Maybe among some humans, too, who wanted to improve themselves."

"Yeah," said Jinx. "What humans do?"

"How about doing it like this?" Freddy said.

"I bet you never saw a mouse
Keeping his hat on in the house.

I bet you never saw a yak
Make faces behind his teacher's back.

I bet you never saw a bear
Put thumbtacks in his father's chair."

"Sure," said Jinx. "That's the way."

"I bet you never saw a cat
Spill gravy on his best cravat."

"I bet you never saw a lion," said Leo,
"When asked to sing, bust out a cryin'."

"*I bet you never saw a moth
Wipe his mouth on the tablecloth,*" put in Jinx.

"*And I bet you never saw a grub
Hit his sister with a club.*"

And Freddy added:

"*I bet you never saw a cow
Using her knife to eat her chow.*

*I bet you never saw a bull
Talking when his mouth was full.*

*I bet you never saw a boar
Precede a lady through a door.*

*I bet you never heard a hornet
Say anything much worse than 'Darn it!'*"

There is no need to continue, since the book, recently published, had, as Freddy had foreseen, an enormous sale among animals. For as Freddy wrote in the *Bean Home News* (he reviewed the book himself): "Never before has it been brought so forcibly to the attention of animals how superior they are to humans. For centuries," he went on, "humans have been telling themselves that they were the kings of the animal kingdom. Yet from the facts gathered together in this book it appears that the so-called lower animals are indeed superior to the self-styled highest. For actions speak louder than words. Without boasting or bragging, let the facts speak for themselves."

Unfortunately, there are always a few, among animals as among humans, who pride themselves on their bad manners. These frequently bought the book as a sort of guide to troublesome behavior. In later editions, therefore, Freddy plans to take out some of the verses which suggest the more unpleasant tricks to play on parents. He feels that the one about thumbtacks was particularly unfortunate, since some animal—he suspects Jinx—planted several of these objects in his study. After sitting on the first two, he of course hunted and found the rest. But the fear of finding others rather spoiled the fun of writing poetry for several weeks.

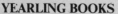
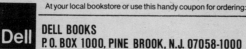

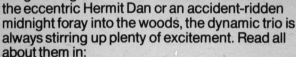